David Garrick, William Wycherley

The Country Girl, a Comedy

(Altered from Wycherley) as it is Acted at the Theatre-Royal in Drury-Lane

David Garrick, William Wycherley

The Country Girl, a Comedy
(Altered from Wycherley) as it is Acted at the Theatre-Royal in Drury-Lane

ISBN/EAN: 9783744793377

Printed in Europe, USA, Canada, Australia, Japan

Cover: Foto ©Andreas Hilbeck / pixelio.de

More available books at **www.hansebooks.com**

THE

COUNTRY GIRL,

A

COMEDY,

(Altered from WYCHERLEY)

As it is Acted at the

Theatre-Royal in *Drury-Lane.*

LONDON:

Printed for T. Becket and P. A. De Hondt, in
the Strand; L. Davis and C. Reymers, in
Holborn; and T. Davies, in Ruffel-Street,
Covent-Garden.

M.DCC.LXVI.

Advertisement.

THE Desire of shewing Miss REYNOLDS to Advantage, was the first Motive for attempting an Alteration of WYCHERLEY'S COUNTRY WIFE. Tho' near half of the following Play is new written, the Alterer claims no Merit, but his Endeavour to clear one of our most celebrated Comedies from Immorality and Obscenity. He thought himself bound to preserve as much of the Original, as could be presented to an Audience of these Times without Offence; and if this Wanton of CHARLES'S

Days

ADVERTISEMENT.

Days is now fo reclaimed, as to become innocent without being infipid,
the prefent Editor will not think his
Time ill employed, which has enabled
him to add fome little Variety to the
Entertainments of the Publick. There
feems indeed an abfolute Neceffity
for reforming many Plays of our moft
eminent Wyiters: For no kind of Wit
ought to be received as an Excufe for
Immorality, nay it becomes ftill more
dangerous in proportion as it is more
witty---Without fuch a Reformation,
our *Englifh* Comedies muft be redu-
ced to a very fmall Number, and
would pall by a too frequent Repetition,
or what is worfe, continue fhamelefs
in fpite of publick Difapprobation.

What-

ADVERTISEMENT.

Whatever fate this Play may have in the Clofet, it is much indebted to the Performers for its favourable Reception upon the Stage.

Dramatis Personæ.

Moody,	*Mr.* HOLLAND.
Harcourt,	*Mr.* PALMER.
Sparkish,	*Mr.* DODD.
Belville,	*Mr.* CAUTHERLY.
Footman,	*Mr.* STRANGE.
Country-Boy,	*Master* BURTON.
Alithea,	*Mrs.* PALMER.
Miss Peggy,	*Miss* REYNOLDS.
Lucy,	*Miss* POPE.

SCENE *London.*

THE

COUNTRY GIRL,

A

COMEDY.

ACT I.

SCENE Harcourt's *lodgings*.

Harcourt *tying up his stockings, and* Belville *sitting by him.*

Harc. HA, ha, ha! and so you are in love, nephew, not reasonably and gallantly, as a young gentleman ought, but sighingly, miserably so—not content to be ankle-deep, you have sous'd over head and ears—ha, Dick?

Belv. I am pretty much in that condition, indeed, uncle.   [*sighs.*

Harc. Nay, never blush at it---when I was of your age, I was asham'd too;---but three years at College, and half a one at Paris, methinks should have cur'd you of that unfashionable weakness---modesty.

Belv. Could I have releas'd myself from that, I had, perhaps, been at this instant happy in the possession of what I must despair now ever to obtain---heigho!

Harc. Ha, ha, ha! very foolish, indeed.

B   *Belv.*

Belv. Don't laugh at me, uncle; I am foolifh, I know; but, like other fools, I deferve to be pitied.

Harc. Prithee don't talk of pity; how can I help you?---for this country girl of yours is certainly married.

Belv. No, no,---I won't believe it; fhe is not married, nor fhe fhan't, if I can help it.

Harc. Well faid, modefty;---with fuch a fpirit you can help yourfelf, Dick, without my affiftance.

Belv. But you muft encourage, and advife me too, or I fhall never make any thing of it.

Harc. Provided the girl is not married; for I never, never encourage young men to covet their neighbours wives.

Belv. My heart affures me, that fhe is not married.

Harc. O to be fure, your heart is much to be rely'd upon---but to convince you that I have a fellow-feeling of your diftrefs, and that I am as nearly ally'd to you in misfortunes as in relationfhip---you muft know---

Belv. What, uncle? you alarm me!

Harc. That I am in love too.

Belv. Indeed!

Harc. Miferably in love.

Belv. That's charming.

Harc. And my miftrefs is juft going to be married to another.

Bel. Better, and better.

Harc. I knew my fellow-fufferings would pleafe you; but now prepare for the wonderful wonder of wonders!

Belv. Well!---

Harc. My miftrefs is in the fame houfe with yours.

Belv. What, are you in love with Peggy too?

[*rifing from his chair.*

Harc.

Harc. Well faid, jealoufy.---No, no, fet your heart at reft.---Your Peggy is too young, and too fimple for me.---I muft have one a little more knowing, a little better bred, juft old enough to fee the difference between me and a coxcomb, fpirit enough to break from a brother's engagements, and chufe for herfelf.

Belv. You don't mean Alithea, who is to be married to Mr. Sparkifh?

Harc. Can't I be in love with a lady that is going to be married to another, as well as you, Sir?

Belv. But Sparkifh is your friend.

Harc. Prithee don't call him my friend; he can be nobody's friend, not even his own---He would thruft himfelf into my acquaintance, would introduce me to his miftrefs, tho' I have told him again and again that I was in love with her, which, inftead of ridding me of him, has made him only ten times more troublefome---and me really in love---He fhould fuffer for his felf-fufficiency.

Belv. 'Tis a conceited puppy!---And what fuccefs with the lady?

Harc. No great hopes,---and yet, if I could defer the marriage a few days, I fhould not defpair; ---her honour, I am confident, is her only attachment to my rival---fhe can't like Sparkifh, and if I can work upon his credulity, a credulity which ev'n popery would be afham'd of, I may yet have the chance of throwing fixes upon the dice to fave me.

Belv. Nothing can fave *me*.

Harc. No, not if you whine and figh, when you fhould be exerting every thing that is man abour you. I have fent Sparkifh, who is admitted at all hours in the houfe, to know how the land lies for you, and if fhe is not married already.

Belv.

Belv. How cruel you are---you'raise me up with one hand, and then knock me down with the other.

Harc. Well, well, she shan't be married. [*knocking at the door.*] This is Sparkish, I suppose; don't drop the least hint of your passion to him; if you do, you may as well advertise it in the publick papers.

Belv. I'll be careful.---

Enter Servant.

Serv. An odd sort of a person, from the country I believe, who calls himself Moody, wants to see you, Sir; but as I did not know him, I said you were not at home, but would return directly; *and so will I too*, said he, very short and surly! and away he went, mumbling to himself.

Harc. Very well, Will.---I'll see him when he comes. [*Exit Servant.*] Moody call to see me! ---He has something more in his head than making me a visit---'tis to complain of you, I suppose.

Belv. How can he know me?

Harc. We must suppose the worst, and be prepared for him---tell me all you know of this ward of his, this Peggy---Peggy what's her name?

Belv. Thrift, Thrift, uncle.

Harc. Ay, ay, Sir Thomas Thrift's daughter, of Hampshire, and left very young, under the guardianship of my old companion and acquaintance, Jack Moody.

Belv. Your companion!---he's old enough to be your father.

Harc. Thank you, nephew---he has greatly the advantage of me in years, as well as wisdom--- When I first launch'd from the university, into this ocean of London---he was the greatest rake in it; I knew him well, for near two years, but all

of

of a fudden he took a freak (a very prudent one)
of retiring wholly into the country.

Belv. There he gain'd fuch an afcendency over
the odd difpofition of his neighbour, Sir Thomas,
that he left him fole guardian to his daughter, who
forfeits half her fortune, if fhe does not marry
with his confent---there's the devil, uncle.

Harc. And are you fo young, fo foolifh, and fo
much in love, that you would take her with half
her value? ha, nephew?

Belv. I'll take her with any thing---with nothing.

Harc. What! fuch an unaccomplifh'd, aukward, filly creature---he has fcarce taught her to
write---fhe has feen nobody to converfe with, but
the country people about 'em; fo fhe can do nothing but dangle her arms, look gawky, turn her
toes in, and talk broad Hampfhire.

Belv. Don't abufe her fweet fimplicity---had
you but heard her talk, as I have done, from the
garden-wall in the country, by moon-light.

Harc. Romeo and Juliet, I proteft, ha, ha, ha!
Arife fair fun, and kill the envious-----ha, ha, ha!
How often have you feen this fair Capulet?

Belv. I faw her three times in the country, and
fpoke to her twice; I have leap'd an orchard-wall,
like Romeo, to come at her, play'd the balcony-
fcene, from an old fummer-houfe in the garden;
and if I lofe her, I will find out an apothecary,
and play the tomb-fcene too, for I cannot bear to
be crofs'd in love.

Harc. Well faid, Dick!---this fpirit muft produce fomething---but has the old dragon ever
caught you fighing at her?

Belv. Never in the country; he faw me yefterday kiffing my hand to her, from the new tavern-
window that looks upon the back of his houfe,

and

and immediately drove her from it, and fasten'd up the window-shutters. ⋅ [*Sparkish without.*

Spark. Very well, Will. I'll go up to 'em.

Harc. I hear Sparkish coming up---take care of what I told you---not a word of Peggy ;---hear his intelligence, and make use of it, without seeming to mind it.

Belv. Mum, mum, uncle.

Enter Sparkish.

Spark. O, my dear Harcourt, I shall die with laughing---I have such news for thee---ha, ha, ha! ---What, your nephew too, and a little dumpish, or so---you have been giving him a lecture upon œconomy, I suppose---you, who never had any, can best describe the evils that arise from the want of it.---I never mind my own affairs, not I.---I hear, Mr. Belville, you have got a pretty snug house, with a bow-window that looks into the Park, and a back-door that goes out into it.--- Very convenient, and well-imagin'd---no young, handsome fellow should be without one---you may be always ready there, like a spider in his web, to seize upon stray'd women of quality.

Harc. As you us'd to do---you vain fellow you ; prithee don't teach my nephew your abandon'd tricks---he is a modest young man, and you must not spoil him.---

Spark. May be so ; but his modesty has done some mischief at our house---my surly, jealous brother-in-law saw that modest young gentleman casting a wishful eye at his forbidden fruit, from the new tavern-window.

Belv. You mistake the person, Mr. Sparkish--- I don't know what young lady you mean.

Harc. Explain yourself, Sparkish, you must mistake---Dick has never seen the girl.

Spark.

Spark. I don't fay he has; I only tell you what *Moody* fays. Befides, he went to the tavern himfelf, and enquir'd of the waiter, who din'd in the back-room,---No. 4,---and they told him it was Mr. Belville, your nephew---that's all I know of the matter, or defire to know of it---faith.

Harc. He kifs'd his hand, indeed, to your lady, Alithea, and is more in love with her than you are, and very near as much as I am ; fo look about you, fuch a youth may be dangerous.

Spark. The more danger the more honour, I defy you both---win her and wear her, if you can ---*Dolus an virtus* in love as well as in war---tho' you muft be expeditious, faith ; for I believe, if I don't change my mind, I fhall marry her tomorrow, or the day after.---Have you no honeft clergyman, Harcourt, no fellow-collegian to recommend to me to do the bufinefs ?

Harc. Nothing ever fure was fo lucky. [*afide.*] Why, faith, I have, Sparkifh---my brother, a twin-brother, Ned Harcourt, will be in town to-day, and proud to attend your commands.---I am a very generous rival, you fee, to lend you my brother to marry the woman I love ?

Spark. And fo am I too, to let your brother come fo near us---but Ned fhall be the man ; poor Alithea grows impatient---I can't put off the evil day any longer-- I fancy the brute, her brother, has a mind to marry his country idiot at the fame time.

Belv. How, country idiot, Sir !

Harc. Taifez vous bete. [*afide to* Belv.] I thought he had been married already.

Spark. No, no, he's not married, that's the joke of it.

Belv. No, no, he is not married.

Harc. Hold your tongue--- [*elbowing* Belville.

Spark.

Spark. Not he---I have the fineſt ſtory to tell you---by the by, he intends calling upon you, for he aſk'd me where you liv'd, to complain of *modeſty* there---He pick'd up an old raking acquaintance of his, as we came along together---Will. Frankly, who ſaw him with his girl, ſculking and muffled up, at the play laſt night---he plagu'd him much about matrimony, and his being aſham'd to ſhew himſelf; ſwore he was in love with his wife, and intended to cuckold him; do you, cry'd Moody, folding his arms, and ſcouling with his eyes thus---*You muſt have more wit than you us'd to have---Beſides, if you have as much as you think you have, I ſhall be out of your reach, and this profligate metropolis, in leſs than a week* ---Moody would fain have got rid of him, but the other held him by the ſleeve, ſo I left 'em; rejoic'd moſt luxuriouſly to ſee the poor devil tormented.

Belv. I thought you ſaid, juſt now, that he was *not* married---is not that a contradiction, Sir?

[Harcourt *ſtill makes ſigns to* Belville.

Spark. Why, it is a kind of one---but conſidering your modeſty, and your ignorance of the young lady, you are pretty tolerably inquiſitive methinks, ha, Harcourt! ha, ha, ha!

Harc. Pooh, pooh! don't talk to that baby, tell me all you know.

Spark. You muſt know, my booby of a brother-in-law hath brought up this ward of his (a good fortune let me tell you) as he coops up, and fattens his chickens, for his own eating---he is plaguy jealous of her, and was very ſorry that he could not marry her in the country, without coming up to town; which he could not do, on account of ſome writings or other; ſo what does my gentleman, he perſuades the poor ſilly girl by breaking a ſix-pence, or ſome nonſenſe or another,

another, that they are to all intents married in
heaven; but that the laws require the figning
of articles, and the church fervice to compleat
their union---fo he has made her call him hufband,
and bud, which fhe conftantly does, and he calls
her wife, and gives out fhe is married, that fhe
may not look after younger fellows nor younger
fellows after her, egad; ha, ha, ha! and all won't do.

Belv. Thank you, Sir---what heav'nly news,
uncle!

Harc. What an idiot you are, nephew! And
fo then you make but one trouble of it; and are
both to be tack'd together the fame day?

Spark. No, no, he can't be married this week;
he damns the lawyers for keeping him in town;---
befides, I am out of favour; and he is continually
fnarling at me, and abufing me, for not being
jealous. [*knocking at the door.*]   There he is---
I muft not be feen with you, for he'll fufpect
fomething; I'll go with your nephew to his houfe,
and we'll wait for you, and make a vifit to my
wife that is to be, and, perhaps, we fhall fhew
young Modefty here a fight of Peggy too.

Enter Servant.

Servt. Sir, here's the ftrange odd fort of a gentleman come again, and I have fhewn him into
the fore-parlour.

Spark. That muft be Moody! well faid, Will.
an odd fort of a ftrange gentleman indeed; we'll
ftep into the next room 'till he comes into this,
and then you may have him all to yourfelf---much
good may do you. [Sparkifh *going, returns.*]
Remember that he is married, or he'll fufpect me
of betraying him.   [*Exit* Sparkifh *and* Belville.

Harc. Shew him up, Will. Now muft I prepare .
myfelf to fee a very ftrange, tho' a very natural
metamorphofis---a once high-fpirited, handfome,
well-

well-drefs'd, raking prodigal of the town, funk into a furly, fufpicious œconomical, country floven ---le voila.

Enter Moody.

Moody. Mr. Harcourt, your humble fervant--- have you forgot me?

Harc. What, my old friend Jack Moody! by thy long abfence from the town, the grumnefs of thy countenance, and the flovenlynefs of thy habit, I fhould give thee joy---you are certainly married.

Moody. My long ftay in the country will excufe my drefs, and I have a fuit of law, that brings me up to town, and puts me out of humour--- befides, I muft give Sparkifh ten thoufand pounds to-morrow to take my fifter off my hands.

Harc. Your fifter is very much obliged to you--- being fo much older than her, you have taken upon you the authority of a father, and have engag'd her to a coxcomb.

Moody. I have, and to oblige her---nothing but coxcombs, or debauchees are the favourites now-a- days, and a coxcomb is rather the more innocent animal of the two.

Harc. She has fenfe, and tafte, and can't like him; fo you muft anfwer for the confequences.

Moody. When fhe is out of my hands, her hufband muft look to confequences. He's a fafhionable fool, and will cut his horns kindly.

Harc. And what is to fecure your worfhip from confequences---I did not expect marriage from fuch a rake---one that knew the town fo well: fye, fye, Jack.

Moody. I'll tell you my fecurity---I have married no London wife.

Harc. That's all one---that grave circumfpection in marrying a country wife, is like refufing a
deceitful,

deceitful, pamper'd, Smithfield-jade, to go and be cheated by a friend in the country.

Moody. I wiſh the devil had both him and his ſimile. [*aſide.*

Harc. Well, never grumble about it, what's done can't be undone; is your wife handſome, and young?

Moody. She has little beauty but her youth, nothing to brag of but her health, and no attrac-. tion but her modeſty---wholeſome, homely, and houſewifely---that's all.

Harc. You talk as like a grazier, as you look, Jack---why did you not bring her to town before, to be taught ſomething?

Moody. Which ſomething I might repent as long as I live---No, no, women and private ſoldiers ſhould be ignorant.

Harc. But prithee why wouldſt thou marry her, if ſhe be ugly, ill-bred, and ſilly? She muſt be rich then.

Moody. As rich, as if ſhe had the wealth of the mogul---ſhe'll not ruin her huſband, like a London-baggage, with a million of vices ſhe never heard of---then becauſe ſhe's ugly, ſhe's the likelier to be my own; and being ill-bred, ſhe'll hate converſation; and ſince ſilly and innocent, will not know the difference between me, and you; that is, between a man of thirty, and one of forty.

Harc. Fifty, to my knowledge---[*Moody turns off, and grumbles.*] But ſee how you and I differ, Jack---wit to me is more neceſſary than beauty: I think no young woman ugly, that has it; and no handſome woman agreeable without it.

Moody. 'Tis my maxim---He's a fool that marries; but he's a greater that does not marry a fool.---I know the town, Mr. Harcourt; and

my

my wife shall be virtuous in spite of you, or your nephew.

Harc. My nephew!---poor sheepish lad---he runs away from every woman he sees---he saw your sister Alithea at the opera, and was much smitten with her---He always toasts her---and hates the very name of Sparkish; I'll bring him to your house---and you shall see what a formidable Tarquin he is.

Moody. I have no curiosity, so give yourself no trouble.---You have heard of a wolf in sheep's cloathing, and I have seen your innocent nephew kissing his hands at my windows.

Harc. At your sister, I suppose; nor at her unless he was tipsy---How can you, Jack, be so outragiously suspicious? Sparkish has promis'd to introduce him to his mistress.

Moody. Sparkish is a fool, and may be, what I'll take care not to be---I confess my visit to you, Mr. Harcourt, was partly for old acquaintance sake, but chiefly to desire your nephew to confine his gallanteries to the tavern, and not send 'em in looks, signs, or tokens, on the other side the way---I keep no brothel----so pray tell your nephew. [*going.*

Harc. Nay, prithee, Jack, leave me in better humour---Well, I'll tell him, ha, ha, ha! poor Dick, how he'll stare. This will give him a reputation, and the girls won't laugh at him any longer. Shall we dine together at the tavern, and send for my nephew to chide him for his gallantry? Ha, ha, ha! we shall have fine sport.

Moody. I am not to be laught out of my senses, Mr. Harcourt---I was once a modest, meek young gentleman myself, and I never have been half so mischievous before or since, as I was in that state of innocence---And so, old friend, make no ceremony with me---I have much business, and you

have

have much pleasure, and therefore, as I hate forms, I will excuse your returning my visit; or sending your nephew to satisfy me of his modesty---and so your servant. [*Exit.*

Harc. [*alone.*] Ha! ha! ha! poor Jack! what a life of suspicion does he lead! I pity the poor fellow, tho' he ought, and will, suffer for his folly---Folly! --- 'tis treason, murder, sacrilege! When persons of a certain age will indulge their false, ungenerous appetites, at the expence of a young creature's happiness, dame nature will revenge herself upon them for thwarting her most heavenly will and pleasure.

END OF THE FIRST ACT.

ACT II.

SCENE *a chamber in* Moody's *house.*

Enter Miss Peggy *and* Alithea.

Peg. PRAY, sister, where are the best fields and woods to walk in, in London?

Alith. A pretty question! why, sister, Vauxhall, Ranelagh, and St. James's Park, are the most frequented.

Peg. Pray, sister, tell me why my Bud looks so grum here in town, and keeps me up close, and will not let me go a walking, nor let me wear my best gown yesterday.

Alith. O, he's jealous, sister.

Peg. Jealous! what's that?

Alith. He's afraid you should love another man.

Peg. How should he be afraid of my loving another man, when he will not let me see any but himself?

Alith. Did he not carry you yesterday to a play?

Peg. Ay; but we sat amongst ugly people: he would not let me come near the gentry, who sat under us, so that I could not see 'em. He told me none but naughty women sat there---but I would have ventur'd for all that.

Alith. But how did you like the play?

Peg. Indeed I was weary of the play; but I lik'd hugeously the actors; they are the goodliest, properest men, sister.

Alith. O, but you must not like the actors, sister.

Peg. Ay, how should I help it, sister? Pray, sister, when my guardian comes in, will you ask leave for me to go a walking?

Alith.

Alith. A walking, ha, ha, ha! Lord, a country gentlewoman's pleasure is the drudgery of a footpost; and she requires as much airing as her husband's horses. [*aside.*

Enter Moody.

But here comes my brother, I'll ask him, tho' I'm sure he'll not grant it.

Peg. O my dear, dear Bud, welcome home; why dost thou look so fropish? who has nanger'd thee?

Moody. You're a fool. [Peggy *goes aside, and cries.*

Alith. Faith, and so she is, for crying for no fault---poor tender creature!

Moody. What, you would have her as impudent as yourself, as arrant a gilflirt, a gadder, a magpye, and, to say all, a mere notorious townwoman!

Alith. Brother, you are my only censurer; and the honour of your family will sooner suffer in your wife that is to be, than in me, tho' I take the innocent liberty of the town.

Moody. Hark you, Mistress, do not talk so before my wife: the innocent liberty of the town!

Alith. Pray, what ill people frequent my lodgings? I keep no company with any woman of scandalous reputation.

Moody. No, you keep the men of scandalous reputation company.

Alith. Would you not have me civil, answer 'em at public places, walk with 'em when they join me in the Park, Ranelagh, or Vauxhall?

Moody. Hold, hold; do not teach my wife where the men are to be found: I believe she's the worse for your town documents already. I bid you keep her in ignorance, as I do.

Peg. Indeed, be not angry with her, Bud, she will tell me nothing of the town, tho' I ask her a thousand times a-day.

Moody.

Moody. Then you are very inquifitive to know, I find ?

Peg. Not I, indeed, Dear ; I hate London : our place-houfe in the country is worth a thoufand of't ; would I were there again.

Moody. So you fhall, I warrant. But were you not talking of plays and players when I came in ? you are her encourager in fuch difcourfes.

Peg. No, indeed, Dear, fhe chid me juft now for liking the player-men.

Moody. Nay, if fhe is fo innocent as to own to me her liking them, there is no hurt in't. [*afide.*] Come, my poor Rogue, but thou likeft none better than me ?

Peg. Yes, indeed, but I do ; the player-men are finer folks.

Moody. But you love none better than me ?

Peg. You are my own dear Bud, and I know you ; I hate ftrangers.

Moody. Ay, my Dear, you muft love me only ; and not be like the naughty town-women, who only hate their hufbands, and love every man elfe, love plays, vifits, fine coaches, fine cloaths, fid-dles, balls, treats, and fo lead a wicked town-life.

Peg. Nay, if to enjoy all thefe things be a town-life, London is not fo bad a place, Dear.

Moody. How ! if you love me, you muft hate London.

Alith. The fool has forbid me difcovering to her the pleafures of the town, and he is now fetting her agog upon them himfelf. [*afide.*]

Peg. But, Bud, do the town-women love the player-men too ?

Moody. Yes, I warrant you.

Peg. Ay, I warrant you.

Moody. Why, you do not, I hope ?

Peg.

Peg.. No, no, Bud; but why have we no player-men in the country?

Moody. Ha! Mrs. Minx, afk me no more to go to a play.

Peg. Nay, why, Love? I did not care for going : but when you forbid me, you make me as 'twere defire it.

Alith. So 'twill be in other things, I warrant.
                                                    [*afide.*

Peg. Pray let me go to a play, Dear?

Moody. Hold your peace, I won't.

Peg. Why, Love?

Moody. Why, I'll tell you.

Alith. Nay, if he tell her, fhe'll give him more caufe to forbid her that place.   [*afide.*

Peg. Pray, why, Dear?

Moody. Firft, you like the actors ; and the gallants may like you.

Peg. What, a homely country girl? No, Bud, no body will like me.

Moody. I tell you yes, they may.

Peg. No, no, you jeft—I won't believe you: I will go.

Moody. I tell you then, that one of the moft raking fellows in town, who faw you there, told me he was in love with you.

Peg. Indeed! who, who, pray, who was't?

Moody. I've gone too far, and flipt before I was aware. How overjoy'd fhe is.   [*afide.*

Peg. Was it any Hampfhire gallant, any of our neighbours?---Promife you, I am beholden to him.

Moody. I promife you, you lye ; for he wou'd but ruin you, as he has done hundreds.

Peg. Ay, but if he loves me, why fhould he ruin me? anfwer me to that. Methinks he fhou'd not ; I wou'd do him no harm.

Alith. Ha, ha, ha!

C

Moody,

Moody. 'Tis very well; but I'll keep him from doing you any harm, or me, either. But here comes company, get you in, get you in.

Peg. But pray, hufband, is he a pretty gentleman, that loves me?

Moody. In, baggage, in. [*thrufts her in, and fhuts the door.*

Enter Sparkifh, Harcourt, *and* Belville.

Moody. What, all the libertines of the town brought to my lodging, by this eafy coxcomb! 'Sdeath, I'll not fuffer it.

Spark. Here, Belville, do you approve my choice? Dear little rogue, I told you, I'd bring you acquainted with all my friends, the wits.

Moody. Ay, they fhall know her as well as you yourfelf will, I warrant you.

Spark. This is one of thofe, my pretty rogue, that are to dance at your wedding to-morrow, And one you muft make welcome, for he's modeft. [*Belville falutes Alithea.*] Harcourt makes himfelf welcome, and has not the fame foible, tho' of the fame family.

Harc. You are too obliging, Sparkifh.

Moody. And fo he is indeed—the fop's horns will as naturally fprout upon his brows, as mufhrooms upon dunghills.

Harc. This, Mr. Moody, is my nephew you mentioned to me; I would bring him with me, for a fight of him will be fufficient, without poppy or mandragora, to reftore you to your reft.

Belv. I am forry, Sir, that any miftake, or imprudence of mine, fhould have given you any uneafinefs; it was not fo intended, I affure you, Sir.

Moody. It may be fo, Sir, but not the lefs criminal for that—My wife, Sir, muft not be fmirk'd and nodded at from tavern windows; I am a good fhot,

fhot, young gentleman, and don't fuffer magpyes to come near my cherries.

Belv. Was it your wife, Sir?

Moody. What's that to you, Sir,—fuppofe it was my grandmother?

Belv. I would not dare to offend her,—permit me to fay a word in private to you. [*Moody and Belville retire out of fight.*]

Spark. Now old furly is gone, tell me, Harcourt, if thou lik'ft her as well as ever—My dear, don't look down, I fhould hate to have a wife of mine out of countenance at any thing.

Alith. For fhame, Mr. Sparkifh.

Spark. Tell me, I fay, Harcourt, how doft like her? thou haft ftar'd upon her enough to refolve me.

Harc. So infinitely well, that I could wifh I had a miftrefs too, that might differ from her in nothing but her love and engagement to you.

Alith. Sir, Mr. Sparkifh has often told me, that his acquaintance were all wits and railers, and now I find it.

Spark. No, by the univerfe, Madam, he does not rally now; you may believe him; I do affure you he is the honefteft, worthieft, true-hearted gentleman; a man of fuch perfect honour, he would fay nothing to a lady he does not mean.

Harc. Sir, you are fo beyond expectation obliging, that——

Spark. Nay, egad, I am fure you do admire her extremely, I fee it in your eyes.—He does admire you, Madam, he has told me fo a thoufand and a thoufand times---have not you, Harcourt? You do admire her, by the world you do—don't you?

Harc. Yes, above the world, or the moft glorious part of it, her whole fex; and till now, I never thought I fhould have envied you or any man

C 2   about

about to marry : but you have the beſt excuſe to marry I ever knew.

Alith. Nay, now, Sir, I am ſatisfied you are of the ſociety of the wits, and raillers ſince you cannot ſpare your friend, even when he is moſt civil to you ; but the ſureſt ſign is, you are an enemy to marriage, the common butt of every railler.

Harc. Truly, Madam, I was never an enemy to marriage till now, becauſe marriage was never an enemy to me before.

Alith. But why, Sir, is marriage an enemy to you now ? becauſe it robs you of your friend here ? for you look upon a friend married, as one gone into a monaſtery, that is dead to the world.

Harc. 'Tis indeed, becauſe you marry him ; I ſee, Madam, you can gueſs my meaning : I do confeſs heartily and openly, I wiſh it were in my power to break the match ; by heavens I wou'd.

Spark. Poor Frank !

Alith. Wou'd you be ſo unkind to me ?

Harc. No, no, 'tis not becauſe I wou'd be unkind to you.

Spark. Poor Frank, no, egad, 'tis only his kindneſs to me.

Alith. Great kindneſs to you indeed---inſenſible ! Let a man make love to his miſtreſs to his face.

                                                 [*aſide.*

Spark. Come, dear Frank, for all my wife there, that ſhall be, thou ſhalt enjoy me ſometimes, dear rogue: by my honour, we men of wit condole for our deceaſed brother in marriage, as much as for one dead in earneſt : I think that was prettily ſaid of me, ha, Harcourt ?—But come, Frank, be not melancholy for me.

Harc. No, I aſſure you, I am not melancholy for you.

Spark. Prithee, Frank, do'ſt think my wife, that ſhall be, there, a fine perſon ?

                                              Harc.

Harc. I cou'd gaze upon her, till I became as blind as you are.

Spark. How, as I am? how?

Harc. Because you are a lover, and true lovers are blind, stock blind.

Spark. True, true; but by the world she has wit too, as well as beauty: go, go with her into a corner, and try if she has wit; talk to her any thing, she's bashful before me.

Alith. Sir, you dispose of me a little before your time. [*aside to Sparkish.*

Spark. Nay, nay, Madam, let me have an earnest of your obedience, or—go, go Madam.
[Harc. *courts* Alithea *aside.*

Enter Moody.

Moody. How, Sir, if you are not concern'd for the honour of a wife, I am for that of a sister; be a pander to your own wife, bring men to her, let 'em make love before your face, thrust 'em into a corner together, then leave 'em in private! is this your town wit and conduct?

Spark. Ha, ha, ha! a silly wise rogue wou'd make one laugh more than a stark fool, ha, ha, ha! I shall burst. Nay, you shall not disturb 'em; I'll vex thee, by the world. What have you done with Belville?
[*Struggles with* Moody *to keep him from* Harcourt *and* Alithea.

Moody. Shewn him the way out of my house, as you should to that gentleman.

Spark. Nay, but prithee—let me reason with thee. [*Talks apart with* Moody.

Alith. The writings are drawn, Sir, settlements made, 'tis too late, Sir, and past all revocation.

Harc. Then so is my death.

Alith. I wou'd not be unjust to him.

Harc. Then why to me so?

C 3   *Alith.*

Alith. I have no obligation to you.

Harc. My love.

Alith. I had his before.

Harc. You never had it; he wants, you fee, jealoufy, the only infallible fign of it.

Alith. Love proceeds from efteem; he cannot diftruft my virtue; befides, he loves me, or he wou'd not marry me.

Harc. Marrying you, is no more a fign of his love, than bribing your woman, that he may marry you, is a fign of his generofity. But if you take marriage for a fign of love, take it from me immediately.

Alith. No, now you have put a fcruple in my head; but in fhort, Sir, to end our difpute, I muft marry him; my reputation wou'd fuffer in the world elfe.

Harc. No; if you do marry him, with your pardon, Madam, your reputation fuffers in the world.

Alith. Nay, now you are rude, Sir—Mr. Sparkifh, pray come hither, your friend here is very troublefome, and very loving.

Harc. Hold, hold.　　　[*afide to Alithea.*

Moody. D'ye hear that?—fenfelefs puppy!

Spark. Why, d'ye think I'll feem jealous, like a country bumkin?

Moody. No, rather be difhonour'd like a credulous driv'ler.

Harc. Madam, you wou'd not have been fo little generous as to have told him?

Alith. Yes, fince you cou'd be fo little generous as to wrong him.

Harc. Wrong him, no man can do't, he's beneath an injury; a bubble, a coward, a fenfelefs idiot, a wretch fo contemptible to all the world but you, that—

Alith.

Alith. Hold, do not rail at him, for fince he is like to be my hufband, I am refolv'd to like him: nay, I think I am oblig'd to tell him, you are not his friend —Mr. Sparkifh, Mr. Sparkifh!

Spark. What, what; now, dear rogue, has not fhe wit?'

Harc. Not fo much as I thought, and hoped fhe had. *[furlily.*

Alith. Mr. Sparkifh, do you bring people to rail at you?

Harc. Madam!

Spark. How! no; but if he does rail at me, 'tis but in jeft, I warrant: what we wits do for one another, and never take any notice of it.

Alith. He fpoke fo fcurriloufly of you, I had no patience to hear him.

Moody. And he was in the right on't.

Alith. Befides, he has been making love to me.

Moody. And I told the fool fo —

Harc. True, damn'd tell-tale woman. *[afide.*

Spark. Pfhaw, to fhew his parts—We wits rail and make love often, but to fhew our parts; as we have no affections, fo we have no malice, we—

Moody. Did you ever hear fuch an afs!

Alith. He faid you were a wretch below an injury.

Spark. Pfhaw.

Harc. Madam!

Alith. A common bubble.

Spark. Pfhaw.

Alith. A coward!

Spark. Pfhaw, pfhaw!

Alith. A fenfelefs drivelling idiot.

Moody. True, true, true; all true.

Spark. How did he difparage my parts? nay, then my honour's concern'd. I can't put up that, Sir; by the world, brother, help me to kill him.

[offers to draw.

Alith. Hold, hold.

Spark. What, what?

Alith.

Alith. I muſt not let 'em kill the gentleman neither. [*aſide.*

Spark. I'll be thy death. [*putting up his ſword.*

Moody. If Harcourt would but kill Sparkiſh, and run away with my ſiſter, I ſhou'd be rid of three plagues at once.

Alith. Hold, hold; indeed, to tell the truth, the gentleman ſaid, after all, that what he ſpoke, was but out of friendſhip to you.

Spark. How! ſay, I am a fool, that is no wit, out of friendſhip to me?

Alith. Yes, to try whether I was concern'd enough for you; and made love to me only to be ſatisfy'd of my virtue, for your ſake.

Harc. Kind, however. [*aſide.*

Spark. Nay, if it were ſo, my dear rogue, I aſk thee pardon; but why wou'd not you tell me ſo, faith?

Harc. Becauſe I did not think on't, faith!

Spark. Come, Belville is gone away; Harcourt, let's be gone to the new play—Come, Madam.

Alith. I will not go, if you intend to leave me alone in the box, and run all about the houſe as you uſe to do.

Spark. Pſhaw, I'll leave Harcourt with you in the box, to entertain you, and that's as good; if I ſat in the box, I ſhou'd be thought no critick—I muſt run about, my dear, and abuſe the author —Come away, Harcourt, lead her down. B'ye, brother. [*Exit Harc. Spark. Alithea.*

Moody. B'ye, driv'ler; well, go thy ways, for the flower of the true town fops, ſuch as ſpend their eſtates before they come to 'em, and are cuckolds before they're married. But let me go look to my free-hold.

Enter a Servant Boy.

Maſter, your worſhip's ſervant—here is the lawyer, counſeller gentleman, with a green bag full

full of papers, come again, and would be glad to
speak to you.

Moody. Now, here's some other damn'd impedi-
ment, which the law has thrown in our way—I
shall never marry the girl, nor get clear of the
smoke and wickedness of this cursed town; where is
he ? [*Exit.*

Boy. He's below in a coach, with three other
lawyer, counseller gentlemen.

S C E N E *changes.*

Enter Miss Peggy *and* Lucy.

Lucy. What ails you, Miss Peggy ? you are
grown quite melancholy.

Peg. Would it not make any one melancholy to
see your mistress Alithea go every day fluttering
about abroad to plays and assembles, and I know
not what, whilst I must stay at home, like a poor
lonely sullen bird in a cage ?

Lucy. Dear Miss Peggy, I thought you chose
to be confin'd : I imagin'd that you had been bred
so young to the cage, that you had no pleasure
in flying about, and hopping in the open air, as
other young ladies who go a little wild about this
town.

Peg. Nay, I confess, I was quiet enough, 'till
somebody told me what pure lives the London
ladies lead, with their dancing meetings, and
junketings, and dress'd every day in their best
gowns ; and I warrant you play at nine-pins every
day in the week, so they do.

Lucy. To be sure, Miss, you will lead a better
life when join'd in holy wedlock with your sweet-
temper'd guardian, the chearful Mr. Moody.

Peg. I can't lead a worse, that's one good
thing—but I must make the best of a bad market,
for I can't marry nobody else.

Lucy.

Lucy. How fo, Mifs? that's very ftrange.

Peg. Why we have a contraction to one ano-the---fo we are as good as married, you know---

Lucy. I know it! Heav'n forbjd, Mifs---

Peg. Heigho!

Lucy. Don't figh, Mifs Peggy—if that young gentleman, who was here juft now, would take pity on me, I'd throw fuch a contract as yours behind the fire.

Peg. Lord blefs us, how you talk!

Lucy. Young Mr. Belville wou'd make you talk otherwife, if you knew him.

Peg. Mr. Belville!---where is he?—when did you fee him?---you have undone me, Lucy—where was he? did he fay any thing?

Lucy. Say any thing! very little, indeed—he's quite diftracted, poor young creature. He was talking with your guardian juft now.

Peg. The duce he was!—but where was it, and when was it?

Lucy. In this houfe, five minutes ago, when your guardian turn'd you into your chamber, for fear of your being feen.

Peg. I knew fomething was the matter, I was in fuch a flufter—but what did he fay to my Bud?

Lucy. What do you call him Bud for? Bud means hufband, and he is not your hufband yet---and I hope never will be—and if he was my hufband, I'd bud him, a furly unreafonable beaft.

Peg. I'd call him any names, to keep him in good humour---if he'd let me marry any body elfe (which I can't do) I'd call him hufband as long as he liv'd—But what faid Mr. Belville to him?

Lucy. I don't know what he faid to him, but I'll tell you what he faid to me, with a figh, and his hand upon his breaft as he went out of the door---If you ever were in love, young gentlewo-

2

man,

man, (meaning me) and can pity a moſt faithful
lover—tell the dear objeƈt of my affeƈtions---

Peg. Meaning me, Lucy?

Lucy. Yes, you, to be ſure. Tell the dear objeƈt
of my affeƈtions, I live but upon the hopes that
ſhe is not married; and when thoſe hopes leave me---
ſhe knows the reſt---then he caſt up his eyes thus---
gnaſh'd his teeth---ſtruck his forehead---would have
ſpoke again, but could not---fetch'd a deep ſigh,
and vaniſh'd.

Peg. That is really very fine---I'm ſure it makes
my heart ſink within me, and brings tears into my
eyes---O he's a charming ſweet---but huſh, huſh, I
hear my huſband!

Lucy. Don't call him huſband. Go into the Park
this evening, if you can.

Peg. Mum, mum---

Enter Moody.

Moody. Come, what's here to do? you are putting the town pleaſures in her head, and ſetting her
a longing.

Lucy. Yes, after nine-pins: you ſuffer none to
give her thoſe longings you mean, but yourſelf.

Moody. Come, Mrs. Flippant, good precepts
are loſt when bad examples are ſtill before us: the
liberty your miſtreſs takes abroad makes her hanker after it, and out of humour at home: poor
wretch! ſhe deſired not to come to London; I
would bring her.

Lucy. O yes, you ſurfeit her with pleaſures.

Moody. She has been this fortnight in town, and
never deſired, till this afternoon, to go abroad.

Lucy. Was ſhe not at the play yeſterday?

Moody. Yes; but ſhe ne'er aſk'd me: I was
myſelf the cauſe of her going.

Lucy. Then if ſhe aſk you again, you are the
cauſe of her aſking, and not my miſtreſs.

Moody.

Moody. Well, next week I fhall be rid of you all, rid of this town, and my dreadful apprehenfions. Come, be not melancholy, for thou fhalt go into the country very foon, deareft.

Lucy. Great comfort!

Peg. Pifh, what d'ye tell me of the country for.

Moody How's this! what, pifh at the country?

Peg. Let me alone, I am not well.

Moody. O, if that be all---what ails my deareft?

Peg. Truly, I don't know ; but I have not been well fince you told me there was a gallant at the play in love with me.

Moody. Ha!

Lucy. That's my miftrefs too.

Moody. Nay, if you are not well, but are fo concern'd, becaufe a raking fellow chanced to lye, and fay he lik'd you, you'll make me fick too.

Peg. Of what ficknefs?

Moody. O, of that which is worfe than the plague, jealoufy.

Peg. Pifh, you jeer: I'm fure there's no fuch difeafe in our receipt book at home.

Moody. No, thou never met'ft with it, poor innocent.

Peg. Well, but pray, Bud, let's go to a play to night.

Moody. No, no;---no more plays---But why are you fo eager to fee a play?

Peg. Faith, Dear, not that I care one pin for their talk there; but I like to look upon the player-men, and wou'd fee, if I could, the gallant you fay loves me: that's all, dear Bud.

Moody. Is that all, dear Bud?

Lucy. This proceeds from my miftrefs's example.

Peg. Let's go abroad however, dear Bud, if we don't go to the play.

Moody. Come, have a little patience, and thou fhalt go into the country next week.

Peg.

Peg. Therefore I would fee firft fome fights, to tell my neighbours of: nay, 1 will go abroad, that's once.

Moody. What, you have put this into her head?

Lucy. Heav'n defend me, what fufpicions! fomebody has put more things into your head than you ought to have.

Moody. Your tongue runs too glibly, Madam, and you have liv'd too long with a London lady, to be a proper companion for innocence---I am not overfond of your miftrefs.

Lucy. There's no love loft between us.

Moody. You admitted thofe gentlemen into the houfe, when I faid I wou'd not be at home; and there was the young fellow too that behav'd fo indecently to my wife at the tavern window.

Lucy. Becaufe you wou'd not let him fee your handfome wife out of your lodgings.

Peg. Why, O Lord! did the gentleman come hither to fee me indeed?

Moody. No, no, you are not the caufe of that damn'd queftion too.

Peg. Come, pray, Bud, let's go abroad before 'tis late; for I will go, that's flat and plain---only into the Park.

Moody. So! the obftinacy already of the town-wife; and I muft, whilft fhe's here, humour her like one. [*afide.*] How fhall we do, that fhe may not be feen or known?

Lucy. Muffle her up with a bonnet and handker-chief, and I'll go with her to avoid fufpicion.

Moody. And run into more danger.---No, no, I am obliged to you for your kindnefs, but fhe fhan't ftir without me.

Lucy. What will you do then?

Peg. What, fhall we go? I am fick with ftaying at home: if I don't walk in the Park, I'll do no-thing that I am bid for a week---I won't be mop'd.

Lucy.

Lucy. O, she has a charming spirit! I could stand your friend now, and would, if you had ever a civil word to give me.

Moody. I'll give thee a better thing, I'll give thee a guinea for thy good advice; if I like it; and I can have the best of the College for the same money.

Lucy. I despise a bribe---when I am your friend, it shall be without fee or reward.

Peg. Don't be long then, for I will go out.

Lucy. The taylor brought home last night the clothes you intend for a present to your godson in the country.

Peg. You must not tell that, Lucy.

Lucy. But I will, Madam---When you were with your lawyers last night, Miss Peggy, to divert me and herself, put 'em on, and they fitted her to a hair.

Moody. Thank you, thank you, Lucy---'tis the luckiest thought! Go this moment, Peggy, into your chamber, and put 'em on again---and you shall walk with me into the Park, as my godson---Well thought of, Lucy---I shall love you for ever for this.

Peg. And so shall I too, Lucy, I'll put 'em on directly. [*going, returns.*] Suppose, Bud, I must keep on my petticoats, for fear of shewing my legs?

Moody. No, no, you fool, never mind your legs.

Peg. No more I will then, Bud---This is pure.
[*Exit rejoiced.*

Moody. What a simpleton it is! Well, Lucy, I thank you for the thought, and before I leave London, thou shalt be convinc'd how much I am obliged to thee.   [*Exit smiling.*

Lucy. And before you leave London, Mr. Moody, I hope I shall convince you how much you are oblig'd to me.   [*Exit.*

END OF THE SECOND ACT.

ACT III.

SCENE *the Park*.

Enter Belville, *and* Harcourt.

Belv. AND the moment Moody left me, and before I left his lodgings, I took an opportunity of conveying some tender sentiments thro' Lucy to Miss Peggy, and it was Lucy advis'd me to ftrole here this evening;—and here I am, in expectation of feeing my country goddefs.

Harc. And fo to blind Moody, and take him off the fcent of your paffion for this girl, and at the fame time to give me an opportunity with Sparkifh's miftrefs, (and of which I have made the moft) you hinted to him with a grave melancholy face, that you were dying for his fifter---gad-a-mercy, nephew! I will back thy modefty againft any other in the three kingdoms---It will do, Dick.

Belv. What could I do, uncle?---it was my laft ftake, and I play'd for a great deal.

Harc. You miftake me, Dick,---I don't fay you could do better---I only can't account for your modefty's doing fo much; you have done fuch wonders, that I, who am rather bold than fheepifh, have not yet ceas'd wondering at you. But do you think that you impos'd upon him?

Belv. Faith, I can't fay---I am rather doubtful, he faid very little, grumbled much, fhook his head, and fhew'd me the door.---But what fuccefs have you had with Alithea?

Harc. Juft enough to have a glimmering of hope, without having light enough to fee an inch
before

before my nofe.---This day will produce fomething; Alithea is a woman of great honour, and will facrifice her happinefs to it, unlefs Sparkifh's abfurdity ftand my friend, and does every thing that the fates ought to do for me.

Belv. Yonder comes the prince of coxcombs, and if your miftrefs and mine fhould, by chance, be tripping this way, this fellow will fpoil fport--- let us avoid him---you can't cheat him before his face.

Harc. But I can tho', thanks to my wit, and his want of it; a foolifh rival, and a jealous hufband, affift their rivals defigns, for they are fure to make their women hate them, which is their firft ftep to their love for another man.

Belv. But you cannot come near his miftrefs but in his company.

Harc. Still the better for me, nephew, for fools are moft eafily cheated, when they themfelves are acceffaries, and he is to be bubbled of his miftrefs, or of his money (the common miftrefs) by keeping him company.

Enter Sparkifh.

Spark. Who's that is to be bubbled? faith, let me fnack; I han't met with a bubble fince Chriftmas. 'Gad, I think bubbles are like their brother woodcocks, go out with the cold weather.

Harc. O pox, he did not hear all, I hope?

[*apart to* Belville.

Spark. Come, you bubbling rogues you, where do we fup? O Harcourt, my miftrefs tells me, you have made love, fierce love to her laft night, all the play long, ha, ha, ha! but I---

Harc. I make love to her!———

Spark. Nay, I forgive thee, and I know her, but I am fure I know myfelf.

Belv.

Belv. Do you, Sir? Then you are the wifeſt man in the world, and I honour you as ſuch. [*bowing.*

Spark. O, your ſervant, Sir, you are at your raillery, are you?---You can't oblige me more---I'm your man---He'll meet with his match---Ha! Harcourt!---Did not you hear me laugh prodigiouſly at the play laſt night?

Harc. Yes, and was very much diſturb'd at it.—You put the actors and audience into confuſion---and all your friends out of countenance.

Spark. So much the better---I love confuſion---and to ſee folks out of countenance;---I was in tip top ſpirits, faith, and ſaid a thouſand good things.

Belv. But I thought you had gone to plays to laugh at the poet's good things, and not at your own?

Spark. Your ſervant, Sir: no, I thank you. 'Gad I go to a play, as to a country treat: I carry my own wine to one, and my own wit to t'other, or elſe I'm ſure I ſhould not be merry at either: and the reaſon why we are ſo often louder than the players, is, becauſe we hate authors damnably.

Belv. But why ſhould you hate the poor rogues? you have too much wit, and deſpiſe writing, I'm ſure.

Spark. O yes, I deſpiſe writing. But women! women, that make men do all fooliſh things, make 'em write ſongs too. Every body does it: 'Tis e'en as common with lovers, as playing with fans; and you can no more help rhyming to your Phillis, than drinking to your Phillis.

Harc. But the poets damn'd your ſongs, did they?

Spark. O yes, damn the poets; they turn'd them into burleſque, as they call it: That burleſque is a hocus pocus trick they have got, which by the virtue of hictius doctius, topſey turvey, they make a clever witty thing abſolute nonſenſe; do

you

you know, Harcourt, that they ridicul'd my laſt ſong, *twang, twang*, the beſt I ever wrote ?

Harc. That may be, and be very eaſily ridicul'd for all that.

Belv. Favour me with it, Sir, I never heard

Spark. What, and have all the Park about us ?

Harc. Which you'll not diſlike, and ſo prithee begin.

Spark. I never am aſk'd twice---and ſo have at you.

S O N G.

I.

Tell not me of the roſes, and lillies,
Which tinge the fair cheek of your Phillis,
Tell not me of the dimples, and eyes,
For which ſilly Corydon dies ;
Let all whining lovers go hang,
My heart would you hit,
Tip your arrow with wit,
And it comes to my heart with a twang, twang,
And it comes to my heart with a twang.

II.

I am rock to the handſome, and pretty,
Can only be touch'd by the witty ;
And beauty will ogle in vain,
The way to my heart's thro' my brain,
Let all whining lovers go hang,
We wits, you muſt know,
Have two ſtrings to our bow,
To return them their darts with a twang, twang,
And return them their darts with a twang.

At

At the end of the song Harcourt *and* Belville *steal away from* Sparkish, *and leave him singing——— He sinks his voice by degrees at the surprise of their being gone; then*

Enter Harcourt *and* Belville.

Spark. What the deuce did you go away for ?
Harc. Your miftrefs is coming.
Spark. The devil fhe is---O hide, hide me from
      her.   [*hides behind* Harcourt.
Harc. She fees you.
Spark. But I will not fee her: for I'm engag'd,
and at this inftant.   [*looking at his watch.*
Harc. Pray firft take me, and reconcile me
to her.
Spark. Another time: faith, it is to a lady,
and one cannot make excufes to a woman.
Belv. You have need of 'em I believe.
Spark. Pfhaw, prithee hide me.

Moody, Peggy, *and* Alithea *appear.*

Harc. Your fervant, Mr. Moody.
Moody. Come along—   [*to* Peggy.
Peg. Lau!---what a fweet delightful place this is!
Moody. Come along, I fay---don't ftare about
you fo---you'll betray yourfelf---
      [*Exit* Moody *pulling* Peggy, Alithea *following.*
Harc. He does not know us—
Belv. Or he won't know us———
Spark. So much the better———
            [*Exit* Belville *after them at a diftance.*
Harc. Who is that pretty youth with him,
Sparkifh ?
Spark. Some relation of Peggy's, I fuppofe, for
he is fomething like her in face and gawkynefs.

D 2   Belville

Belville *returns.*

Belv. By all my hopes, uncle---Peggy in man's clothes---I am all over agitation.   [*afide to* Harc.

Harc. Be quiet, or you'll fpoil all. They return--- Alithea has feen you, Sparkifh, and will be angry if you don't go to her: befides, I wou'd fain be reconcil'd to her, which none but you can do, my dear friend.

Spark. Well, that's a better reafon, dear friend: I wou'd not go near her now for her's or my own fake; but I can deny you nothing: for tho' I have known thee a great while, never go, if I do not love thee as well as a new acquaintance.

Harc. I am obliged to you indeed, my dear friend: I wou'd be well with her, only to be well with thee ftill; for thefe ties to wives ufually diffolve all ties to friends.

Spark. But they fhan't tho'---come along.

[*they retire.*

Re-enter Moody *and* Peggy *in man's clothes,* Alithea *following.*

Moody. Sifter, if you will not go, we muft leave you---[*to* Alithea.] The fool her gallant and fhe will mufter up all the young faunterers of this place. What a fwarm of cuckolds and cuckold-makers are here? I begin to be uneafy. [*afide.*] Come, let's be gone, Peggy.

Peg. Don't you believe that I han't half my bellyful of fights yet?

Moody. Then walk this way.

Peg. Lord, what a power of fine folks are here. And Mr. Belville, as I hope to be married. [*afide.*

Moody. Come along; what are you a muttering at?

Peg.

Peg. There's the young gentleman there, you were so angry about—that's in love with me.

Moody. No, no, he's a dangler after your sister—or pretends to be---but they are all bad alike---come along, I say.　　*[he pulls her away.*

Peg. I'm glad to hear that---perhaps I may fit you tho'.　*[Exit with* Moody, Belville *eyeing them.*

Sparkish, Harcourt, Alithea, *come forward.*

Spark. Come, dear Madam, for my sake you shall be reconciled to him.

Alith. For your sake I hate him.

Harc. That's something too cruel, Madam, to hate me, for his sake.

Spark. Ay, indeed, Madam, too, too cruel to me, to hate my friend for my sake.

Alith. I hate him, because he is your enemy; and you ought to hate him too, for making love to me, if you love me.

Spark. That's a good one! I hate a man for loving you! If he did love you, 'tis but what he can't help; and 'tis your fault, not his, if he admires you.

Alith. Is it for your honour, or mine, to suffer a man to make love to me, who am to marry you to-morrow?

Harc. But why, dearest Madam, will you be more concern'd for his honour than he is himself? Let his honour alone for my sake and his. He has no honour.

Spark. How's that?

Harc. But what, my dear friend, can guard himself.

Spark. O ho—that's right again.

Alith.

Alith. You aftonifh me, Sir, with want of jealoufy.

Spark. And you make me giddy, Madam, with your jealoufy and fears, and virtue and honour: 'Gad, I fee virtue makes a woman as troublefome as a little reading or learning.

Harc. Come, Madam, you fee you ftrive in vain to make him jealous of me : my dear friend is the kindeft creature in the world to me.

Spark. Poor fellow.

Harc. But his kindnefs only is not enough for me, without your favour, your good opinion, dear Madam : 'tis that muft perfect my happinefs. Good gentleman, he believes all I fay : wou'd you wou'd do fo. Jealous of me ! I wou'd not wrong him nor you for the world.

Spark. Look you there: hear him, hear him, and not walk away fo.   Come back again.
              [Alithea *walks carelefly to and fro.*

Harc. I love you, Madam, fo———

Spark. How's that! nay—now you begin to go too far indeed.

Harc. So much, I confefs, I fay, I love you, that I wou'd not have you miferable, and caft yourfelf away upon fo unworthy and inconfiderable a thing, as what you fee here.
              [*Clapping his hand on his breaft, points to* Sparkifh.

Spark. No, faith, I believe thou wou'dft not ; now his meaning is plain; but I knew before thou wou'dft not wrong me, nor her.

Harc. No, no, heav'ns forbid the glory of her fex fhou'd fall fo low, as into the embraces of fuch a contemptible wretch, the leaft of mankind---my dear friend here---I injure him.

Alith. Very well.   [*embracing* Sparkifh.

Spark. No, no, dear friend, I knew it: Madam, you fee he will rather wrong himfelf than me in giving himfelf fuch names.

Alith. Do not you underftand him yet ?

                                         Spark.

Spark. Come, come, you fhall ftay till he has faluted you; that I may be affur'd you are friends, after his honeft advice and declaration: come, pray, Madam, be friends with him.

Enter Moody *and* Peggy. Belville *at a diftance.*

Alith. You muft pardon me, Sir, that I am not yet fo obedient to you.

Moody. What, invite your wife to kifs men? Monftrous! Are you not afham'd? I will never forgive you. Let's be gone, fifter.

Spark. Are you not afham'd, that I fhou'd have more confidence in the chaftity of your family, than you have?----You muft not teach me, I am a man of honour, Sir, tho' I am frank and free; I am frank, Sir---

Moody. Very frank, Sir, to fhare your wife with your friends---You feem to be angry and yet won't go.   [*to* Alithea.

Alith. No impertinence fhall drive me away.

Moody. Becaufe you like it---But you ought to blufh at expofing your wife as you do.

Spark. What then? It may be I have a pleafure in't, as I have to fhow fine clothes at a play-houfe, the firft day, and count money before poor rogues.

Moody. He that fhews his wife, or money, will be in danger of having them borrowed fometimes.

Spark. I love to be envy'd, and wou'd not marry a wife, that I alone cou'd love. Loving alone is as dull as eating alone; and fo good night, for I muft to Whitehall---Madam, I hope, you are now reconcil'd to my friend; and fo I wifh you a good night, Madam, and fleep if you can; for to-morrow you know I muft vifit you early with a canonical gentleman. Good night, dear Harcourt---remember to fend your brother. [*Exit* Sparkifh.

Harc. You may depend upon me. Madam, I hope you will not refufe my vifit to-morrow, if it fhould be earlier, with a canonical gentleman, than Mr. Sparkifh.

Moody. This gentlewoman is yet under my care, therefore you muft yet forbear your freedom with her. [*coming between* Alithea *and* Harcourt.

Harc. Muft, Sir !

Moody. Yes, Sir, fhe is my fifter.

Harc. 'Tis well fhe is, Sir----for I muft be her fervant, Sir.---Madam---

Moody. Come away, fifter, we had been gone if it had not been for you, and fo avoided thefe lewd rake-hells, who feem to haunt us.

Harc. I fee a little time in the country makes a man turn wild and unfociable, and only fit to converfe with his horfes, dogs, and his herds.

Moody. I have bufinefs, Sir, and muft mind it: your bufinefs is pleafure, therefore you and I muft go diff'rent ways.

Harc. Well, you may go on; but this pretty young gentleman [*takes hold of* Peggy] fhall ftay with us, for I fuppofe his bufinefs is the fame with ours, pleafure.

Moody. 'Sdeath, he knows her, fhe carries it fo fillily; yet if he does not, I fhou'd be more filly to difcover it firft. [*afide.*

Alith. Pray, let him go, Sir.

Moody. Come, come.

Harc. Had you not rather ftay with us? [*to* Peggy.] Prithee who is this pretty young fellow ?

Moody. One to whom I am a guardian---I wifh I cou'd keep her out of your hands. [*afide.*

Harc.

Harc. Who is he? I never faw any thing fo pretty in all my life.

Moody. Pfhaw, do not look upon him fo much, he's a poor bafhful youth, you'll put him out of countenance.   [*offers to take her away.*

Harc. Here, nephew---let me introduce this young gentleman to your acquaintance---You are very like, and of the fame age, and fhould know one another---Salute him, Dick, a la Francoife.
                    [Belville *kiffes her.*

Moody. I hate French fafhions. Men kifs one another.   [*Endeavours to take hold of her.*

Peg. I am out of my wits---What do you kifs me for ? I am no woman.

Harc. But you are ten times handfomer.

Peg. Nay, now you jeer one; and pray don't jeer me.

Harc. Kifs him again, Dick.

Moody. No, no, no ; come away, come away.
                    [*to* Peggy.

Harc. Why, what hafte are you in ? Why won't you let me talk with him ?

Moody. Becaufe you'll debauch him, he's yet young and innocent. How fhe gazes upon him ! The devil! [*afide.*] Come, pray let him go, I cannot ftay fooling any longer; I tell you my wife ftays fupper for us.

Harc. Does fhe ? Come then, we'll all go fup with her.

Moody. No, no---now I think on't, having ftaid fo long for us, I warrant fhe's gone to bed---I wifh fhe and I were well out of your hands. [*afide.*] Come, I muft rife early to morrow ; come---

Harc. Well then, if fhe be gone to bed, I wifh her and you a good night. But pray, young gentleman, prefent my humble fervice to her.

Peg. Thank you heartily, Sir.   [*bowing.*
                                      Moody.

Moody. 'Sdeath, she will difcover herfelf yet in fpite of me.   [*afide.*

Belv. And mine too, Sir.

Peg. That I will, indeed.   [*bowing.*

Harc. Pray give her this kifs for me. [*kiffes* Peggy.

Moody. O heavens ! what do I fuffer ?

Belv. And this for me.

Peg. Thank you, Sir.   [*courtfies.*

Moody. O the idiot---now 'tis out.---Ten thoufand cankers gnaw away their lips. Come, come, Driv'ler.

Harc. Good night, dear little gentleman. Madam, good night---Farewel, Moody---Come, nephew---have not I rais'd his jealous gall finely ?   [*afide to* Belville.

Belv. A little too much I fear.   [*Exit* Harc. *and* Belville.

Moody. So, they are gone at laft. Sifter, ftay with Peggy---'till I find my fervant---don't let her ftir an inch, I'll be back directly.   [*Exit* Moody.

Harcourt *and* Belville *return.*

Harc. What, not gone yet?---Nephew, fhew the young gentleman Rofamond's Pond, while I fpeak another word to this lady.

Belv. Shall I have that pleafure ?

Peg. With all my heart and foul, Sir.
         [*Exit* Belville *and* Peggy.

Alith. I cannot confent to it indeed.

Harc. Let 'em look upon the place where fo many defpairing lovers have been deftroy'd---You muft indulge them---and me too in a few words.
        [Alithea *and* Harcourt *ftruggle.*

Alith. My brother will go diftracted---tho' he deferves to be vex'd a little for his brutality.

               Harc.

Harc. My nephew is a very modeſt young man, you may depend upon his prudence.

Alith. Modeſt, prudent, and your nephew---I can't believe it, and I muſt follow them.--- [*going.*

Enter Moody.

Moody. Where! How!---what's become of---gone---whither ?---

Alith. He's only gone with the young gentleman to ſee ſomething.

Moody. Something! ſee ſomething! with a plague---where are they ?

Alith. In the next walk only, brother.

Moody. Only, only, where, where ?--- [*Exit.*

Harc. What's the matter with him ? Why ſo much concerned ? But, deareſt Madam---

Alith. Pray let me go, Sir; I have ſaid and ſuffer'd enough already.

Harc. Then you will not look upon, nor pity my ſufferings ?

Alith. To look upon 'em, when I cannot help 'em, were cruelty, not pity; therefore I will never ſee you more.

Enter Moody.

Moody. Gone, gone, not to be found; quite gone; ten thouſand plagues go with 'em; which way went they ?

Alith. But in t'other walk, brother.

Moody. T'other walk---t'other devil! You are ſo full of vanity, and fond of admiration, that you'll ſuffer your own honour and mine to run any riſque, rather than not indulge your inordinate deſire of flattery.---Where are they, I ſay ?

Alith. You are too abuſive, brother, and too

violent

violent about trifles; therefore let your jealoufy fearch for them, for I know nothing of 'em.

Moody. You know where they are, you infamous wretch, eternal fhame of your family; which you do not difhonour enough yourfelf, you think, but you muft help her to it too, thou legion of---

Alith. Good brother---

Moody. Falfe, falfe fifter--- [*Exit* Moody.

Alith. Shew me to my chair, Mr. Harcourt--- His fcurrility has overpower'd me---I will get rid of his tyranny and your importunities, and give my hand to Sparkifh to-morrow morning. [*Exeunt.*

SCENE *changes to another part of the Park.*

Enter Belville *and Mifs* Peggy.

Belv. No difguife could conceal you from my heart; I pretended not to know you, that I might deceive the dragon that continually watches over you---but now he's afleep, let us fly from mifery to happinefs.

Peg. Indeed, Mr. Belville, as well as I like you, I can't think of going away with you fo---and as much as I hate my guardian, I muft take leave of him a little handfomely, or he will kill me, fo he will.

Belv. But, dear Mifs Peggy, think of your fituation; if we don't make the beft ufe of this opportunity, we never may have another.

Peg. Ay, but Mr. Belville---I am as good as married already---my guardian has contracted me, and there wants nothing but church ceremony to make us one---I call him hufband, and he calls me wife already: He made me do fo;---and we

had

had been married in church long ago, if the writings could have been finiſh'd.

Belv. That's his deceit, my ſweet creature--- He pretends to have married you, for fear of your liking any body elſe---You have a right to chuſe for yourſelf, and there is no law in heaven or earth that binds you before marriage to a man you cannot like.

Peg. I'fack, no more I believe it does; ſiſter Alithea's maid has told me as much---ſhe's a very ſenſible girl.

Belv. You are in the very jaws of perdition, and nothing but running away can avoid it---the law will finiſh your chains to morrow, and the church will rivet them the day after---Let us ſecure our happineſs by eſcape, and love and fortune will do the reſt for us.

Peg. Theſe are fine ſayings, to be ſure, Mr. Belville; but how ſhall we get my fortune out of Bud's clutches? We muſt be a little cunning, 'tis worth trying for---We can at any time run away without it.

Belv. I ſee by your fears, my dear Peggy, that you live in awe of this brutal guardian; and if he has you once more in his poſſeſſion, both you and your fortune are ſecur'd to him for ever.

Peg. Ay, but it ſhan't, tho'---I thank him for that.

Belv. If you marry without his conſent, he can but ſeize upon half your fortune---The other half, and a younger brother's fortune, with a treaſure of love, are our own---Take it, my ſweeteſt Peggy, and this moment, or we ſhall be divided for ever.

[*kneels and preſſes her hand.*

Peg. Ifackins, but we won't---Your fine talk has bewitch'd me.

Belv. 'Tis you have bewitch'd me---thou dear inchanting ſweet ſimplicity---Let us fly with the

3

wings of love to my houſe there, and we ſhall be
ſafe for ever.

Peg. And ſo we will then---there ſqueeze me
again by the hand; now run away with me, and
if my guardy follows us, the devil take the hind-
moſt, I ſay. [*going.*] Boo!---here he is.

Enter Moody *haſtily, and meets them.*

Belv. Curſt fortune!

Moody. O! there's my ſtray'd ſheep, and the
wolf again in ſheep's cloathing!---Now I have
recover'd her, I ſhall come to my ſenſes again---
Where have you been, you puppy?

Peg. Been, Bud?---We have been hunting all
over the Park to find you.

Belv. From one end to the other, Sir. [*confuſedly.*

Moody. But not where I was to be found, you
young devil you---Why did you ſtart when you
ſaw me?

Peg. I'm always frighten'd when I ſee you, and
if I did not love you ſo well---I ſhould run away
from you, ſo I ſhould.   [*pouting.*

Moody. But I'll take care you don't.

Peg. This gentleman has a favour to beg of
you, Bud.   [Belville *makes ſigns of diſlike.*

Moody. I am not in the humour to grant favours
to young gentlemen, tho' you may.---What have
you been doing with this young lady?---Gentleman
I would ſay,---bliſters on my tongue!

Belv. Fie, Bud, you have told all.

Belv. I have been as civil as I could to the
young ſtranger; and if you'll permit me, I will take
the trouble off your hands, and ſhew the young
ſpark Roſamond's Pond, for he has not ſeen it
yet---Come, pretty youth, will you go with me?
                                   [*goes to her.*

4   *Peg.*

Peg. As my guardian pleafes.

Moody. No, no, it does not pleafe me---whatever I think he ought to fee, I fhall fhow him myfelf---You may vifit Rofamond's Pond if you will---and the bottom of it, if you will---And fo, Sir, your humble fervant. [*Exit with Mifs under his arm.*

Belv. What curfed luck! [*ftamps*] to be prevented at the very inftant of my carrying off the golden fleece!---We have now rais'd his fufpicions to fuch a degree, that he'll lock her up directly---fign articles this night---marry her in the morning---and away from the church into the country.--- What a miferable fituation am I in!---I have love enough to be a knight-errant in the caufe---I will lofe my life, or refcue my Dulcinea.---I have hopes in her fpirit too---for at the worft fhe can open her window, throw herfelf into my arms, from thence into a poft-chaife, and away for the Tweed as faft as love and four poft-horfes can carry us. [*Exit.*

THE END OF THE THIRD ACT.

ACT IV.

SCENE Moody's *house*.

Lucy, Alithea *drefs'd*.

Lucy. WELL, Madam, now I have drefs'd you, and fet you out with fo many ornaments, and fpent fo much time upon you, and all this for no other purpofe but to bury you alive; for I look upon Mr. Sparkifh's bed to be little better than a grave.

Alith. Hold your peace.

Lucy. Nay, Madam, I will afk you the reafon, why you wou'd banifh poor Mr. Harcourt for ever from your fight? how cou'd you be fo hard-hearted?

Alith. 'Twas becaufe I was not hard-hearted.

Lucy. No, no; 'twas ftark love and kindnefs, I warrant?

Alith. It was fo; I wou'd fee him no more, becaufe I love him.

Lucy. Hey day! a very pretty reafon.

Alith. You do not underftand me.

Lucy. I wifh you may yourfelf.

Alith. I was engag'd to marry, you fee, another man, whom my juftice will not fuffer me to deceive or injure.

Lucy. Can there be a greater cheat or wrong done to a man, than to give him your perfon, with-

without your heart? I fhou'd make a confcience
of it.

Alith. I'll retrieve it for him, after I am married.

Lucy. The woman that marries to love better,
will be as much miftaken, as the rake that marries to live better.

Alith. What nonfenfe you talk.

Lucy. 'Tis a melancholy truth, Madam---Mar-
rying to increafe love, is like gaming to become
rich---Alas! you only lofe what little ftock you
had before---There are many woeful examples of
it in this righteous town!

Alith. I find by your rhetorick you have been
brib'd to betray me.

Lucy. Only by his merit, that has brib'd your
heart, you fee, againft your word and rigid honour.

Alith. Come, pray talk no more of honour,
nor Mr. Harcourt; I wifh the other wou'd come
to fecure my fidelity to him, and his right in me.

Lucy. You will marry him then?

Alith. Certainly; I have given him already my
word, and will my hand too, to make it good,
when he comes.

Lucy. Well, I wifh I may never ftick a pin
more, if he be not an errant natural to t'other fine
gentleman.

Alith. I own he wants the wit of Harcourt,
which I will difpenfe withal, for another want he
has, which is want of jealoufy, which men of
wit feldom want.

Lucy. Lord, Madam, what fhou'd you do with
a fool to your hufband? You intend to be honeft,
don't you? Then that hufbandly virtue, credulity,
is thrown away upon you.

Alith. He only that cou'd fufpect my virtue,
fhou'd have caufe to do it; 'tis Sparkifh's confidence in my truth, that obliges me to be faithful
to him.

E   *Lucy.*

Lucy. What, faithful to a creature who is incapable of loving and efteeming you as he ought!---To throw away your beauty, wit, accomplifhments, fweet temper.——

Alith. Hold your tongue.

Lucy. That you know I can't do, Madam; and upon this occafion, I will talk for ever.---What, give yourfelf away to one, that poor I, your maid, would not accept of?

Alith. How, Lucy!

Lucy. I would not, upon my honour, Madam; 'tis never too late to repent.---Take a man, and give up your coxcomb, I fay.

Enter Servant.

Serv. Mr. Sparkifh, with company, Madam, attends you below.

Alith. I will wait upon 'em. [*Exit Servant.*] My heart begins to fail me, but I muft go through with it; go with me, Lucy.   [*Exit.*

Lucy. Not I, indeed, Madam---If you will leap the precipice, you fhall fall by yourfelf.---What excellent advice have I thrown away!---So I'll e'en take it whete it will be more welcome.---Mifs Peggy is bent upon mifchief againft her guardian, and fhe can't have a better privy-counfellor than myfelf---I muft be bufy one way or another. [*Exit.*

SCENE

SCENE *a chamber in* Moody's *houfe.*

Moody *and Mifs* Peggy.

Moody. I faw him kifs your hand, before you faw me. This pretence of liking my fifter was all a blind---the young abandon'd hypocrite! [*afide.*] Tell me, I fay, for I know he likes you, and was hurrying you to his houfe---tell me, I fay---

Peg. Lord, han't I told it a hundred times over?

Moody. I would try if, in the repetition of the ungrateful tale, I cou'd find her altering it in the leaft circumftance, for if her ftory be falfe, fhe is fo too. [*afide.*] Come, how was't, baggage?

Peg. Lord, what pleafure you take to hear it, fure?

Moody. No, you take more in telling it, I find; but fpeak, how was't? no lies---I faw him kifs you ---he kifs'd you before my face.

Peg. Nay, you need not be fo angry with him neither, for, to fay truth, he has the fweeteft breath I ever knew.

Moody. The Devil!---you were fatisfy'd with it then, and would do it again?---

Peg. Not unlefs he fhou'd force me.

Moody, Force you, changeling.

Peg. If I had ftruggled too much, you know--- ne wou'd have known I had been a woman; fo I was quiet, for fear of being found out.

Moody. If you had been in petticoats, you wou'd have knock'd him down, wou'd not you?

Peg. With what, Bud?---I cou'd not help myfelf ---befides, he did it fo modeftly, and blufh'd fo--- that I almoft thought him a girl in men's cloaths, and upon his mummery too as well as me---and if fo, there was no harm done, you know.

Moody. This is worfe and worfe---fo 'tis plain fhe loves him, yet fhe has not love enough to make her conceal it from me; but the fight of him will encreafe her averfion for me, and love for him; and that love inftruct her how to deceive me, and fatisfy him, all idiot as fhe is: Love, 'twas he gave women firft their craft, their art of deluding; out of nature's hands they came plain, open, filly, and fit for flaves, as fhe and heaven intended 'em, but damn'd Love---well---I muft ftrangle that little monfter, whilft I can deal with him.---Go, fetch pen, ink and paper, out of the next room.

Peg. Yes, I will, Bud, what's the matter now? [*afide.*]   [*Exit.*

Moody. This young fellow loves her, and fhe loves him---the reft is all hypocrify---how the young modeft villain endeavoured to deceive me! But I'll crufh this mifchief in the fhell---Why, fhould woman have more invention in love than men? It can only be, becaufe they have more defire, more foliciting paffions, more of the Devil.   [*afide.*

Enter Mifs Peggy.

Come, Minks, fit down and write.

Peg. Ay, dear, dear Bud, but I can't do't very well.

Moody. I wifh you cou'd not at all.

Peg. But what fhould I write for?

Moody. I'll have you write a letter to this young man.

Peg. O Lord, to the young gentleman a letter!

Moody. Yes, to the young gentleman.

Peg. Lord, you do but jeer; fure you jeft.

Moody. I am not fo merry; come, fit down, and write as I bid you.

Peg. What, do you think I am a fool?

Moody. She's afraid I wou'd not dictate any love to him, therefore fhe's unwilling; but you had beft begin.   *Peg.*

Peg. Indeed, and indeed, but I won't, fo I won't.

Moody. Why?

Peg. Becaufe he's in town; you may fend for him here, if you will.

Moody. Very well, you wou'd have him brought to you?—is it come to this? I fay take the pen ink and write, or you'll provoke me.

Peg. Lord, what d'ye make a fool of me.for? Don't I know that letters are never writ, but from the country to London, and from London into the country? now he's in town, and I am in town too; therefore I can't write to him, you know.

Moody. So, I am glad it is no worfe; fhe is inno-cent enough yet. [*afide.*] Yes you may, when your huf-band bids, write letters to people that are in town.

Peg. O may I fo! then I am fatisfied.

Moody. Come begin---*Sir*--- [*dictates.*

Peg. Shan't I fay, *Dear Sir?* you know one fays always fomething more than bare Sir.

Moody. Write as I bid you, or I will write fome-thing with this penknife in your face.

Peg. Nay, good, Bud—*Sir*--- [*writes.*

Moody. *Though I fuffer'd laft night your naufeous loath'd kiffes and embraces*---write!

Peg. Nay, why fhou'd I fay fo? you know I told you he had a fweet breath.

Moody. Write!

Peg. Let me put out *loath'd.*

Moody. Write, I fay.

Peg. Well then. [*writes.*

Moody. Let me fee what have you writ.
Tho' I fuffer'd laft night your kiffes and embraces---
[*reads the paper.*
Thou impudent creature, where is *naufeous* and *loath'd?*

Peg. I can't abide to write fuch filthy words.

Moody. Once more write as I'd have you, and queftion it not, or I will fpoil your writing with

this; I will ftab out thofe eyes that caufe my mifchief.   [*holds up the penknife.*

Peg. O Lord, I will.

Moody. So---fo---let's fee now! *tho' I fuffered
laft night your naufeous loath'd kiffes and embraces;
go on--- yet I would not have you prefume that you
fhall ever repeat them---fo.*   [*fhe writes.*

Peg. I have writ it.

Moody. O then---*I then conceal'd myfelf from your
knowledge, to avoid your infolencies---* [*fhe writes.*

Peg. To avoid---

Moody. *Your infolencies---*

Peg. Your infolencies.   [*writes.*

Moody. *The fame reafon, now I am out of your hands--*

Peg. So---   [*fhe writes.*

Moody. *Makes me own to you my unfortunate—tho'
innocent frolick of being in man's clothes.* [*fhe writes.*

Peg. So---

Moody. *That you may for evermore.*

Peg. Evermore?

Moody. *Evermore ceafe to purfue her, who hates
and detefts you.*   [*fhe writes.*

Peg. So---h.   [*fighs.*

Moody. What do you figh for?---*detefts you---as
much as fhe loves her hufband and her honour---*

Peg. I vow, hufband, he'll ne'er believe I fhou'd
write fuch a letter.

Moody. What, he'd expect a kinder from you?
Come, now your name only.

Peg. What, fhan't I fay your moft faithful
humble fervant till death?

Moody. No, tormenting fiend—Her ftile I find
wou'd be very foft. [*afide.*] Come, wrap it up now,
whilft I go fetch wax and a candle, and write on
the outfide, *For Mr. Belville.*   [*Exit* Moody.

Peg. For Mr. Belville---fo---I am glad he is
gone—Hark! I hear a noife [*goes to the door.*]
ifeck there's folks with him——that's pure——
now I may think a little——Why fhould
                                      I fend

I fend dear Mr. Bellville fuch a letter?—Can one have no fhift? ah! a London woman wou'd have had a hundred prefently.---Stay---what if I fhould write a letter and wrap it up like this, and write upon't too?---Ay, but then my guardian wou'd fee't---I don't know what to do---But yet y'vads I'll try, fo I will---for I will not fend this letter to poor Mr. Belville, come what will on't.

[*fhe writes, and repeats what fhe writes.*]

Dear, fweet, Mr. Belville---fo---*My guardian wou'd have me fend you a bafe, rude letter, but I won't*---fo---*and wou'd have me fay, I hate you*---*but I won't*---there---*for I'm fure if you and I were in the country at cards together*---fo---*I cou'd not help treading on your toe under the table*---*fo pray keep at home, for I fhall be with you as foon as I can*---*fo no more at prefent from me who am, dear, dear, poor, dear Mr. Belville, your loving friend till death, Margaret Thrift.*

So---now wrap it up juft like t'other---fo---now write, *For Mr. Belville*---But oh! what fhall I do with it? for here comes my guardian.

Enter Moody.

Moody. I have been detained by a fparkifh coxcomb, who pretended a vifit to me, but I fear 'twas to my wife. [*afide.*] What have you done?

Peg. Ay, ay, Bud, juft now.

Moody. Let's fee't; what d'ye tremble for?--- [*he opens and reads the firft letter.*

Peg. So I had been ferv'd, if I had given him this. [*afide.*

Moody. Come, where's the wax and feal?

Peg. Lord, what fhall I do now? Nay, then I have it—pray let me fee't. Lord, you think me fo errand a fool, I cannot feal a letter; I will do't,

E 4   fo

fo I will. [*fnatches the letter from him, changes it
for the other, feals it, and delivers it to him.*

Moody. Nay, I believe you will learn that and
other things too, which I wou'd not have you.

Peg. So, han't I done it curioufly? I think I
have—there's my letter going to Mr. Belville,
fince he'll needs have me fend letters to folks. [*afide.*

Moody. 'Tis very well; but I warrant, you wou'd
not have it go now?

Peg. Yes, indeed, but I wou'd, Bud, now.

Moody. Well, you are a good girl then. Come,
let me lock you up in your chamber, till I come
back; and befure you come not within three ftrides
of the window, when I am gone; for I have a fpy
in the ftreet. [*puts her into the chamber.*] At leaft 'tis
fit fhe thinks fo; if we do not cheat women, they'll
cheat us, and fraud may be juftly ufed with fecret
enemies, of which a wife is the moft dangerous;
and he that has a handfome one to keep, and a
frontier town, muft provide againft treachery rather than open force---Now I have fecured all within, I'll deal with the foe without, with falfe intelligence. This will dafh all his impudent hopes,
[*holds up the letter*] at once, and I fhall fleep now
fecurely in my garrifon without fear of furprize---
But no time is to be loft---I'll fteal a march upon
him.   [*Exit.*

SCENE *changes to* Belville's *lodgings.*

Enter Lucy *and* Belville.

Lucy. I run great rifques to be fure to ferve the
young lady, and you, Sir---but I know you are a
gentleman of honour, and wou'd fcorn to betray a
friend who means you well, and is above being
mercenary.

Belv. As you are not mercenary, Mrs. Lucy,
I ought to be the more generous---give me leave
to

to prefent you with this trifle, [*gives a ring.*] not as a reward for fervices, but as a fmall token of friendfhip.

Lucy. Tho' I fcorn to be brib'd in any caufe, yet I am proud to accept it, as a mark of your regard, and as fuch fhall keep it for your fake— and now to bufinefs.

Belv. You flatter me then, that Mifs Peggy has the moft rooted averfion for her guardian, and fome prejudices in my favour.

Lucy. She has intrufted me with her very thoughts—and I have rais'd her difobedience to fuch a pitch, that fhe would have open'd her whole heart to you in a letter, had we not been interrupted by her brutal guardian.

Belv. She told me in the Park, that you had convinced her, fhe was not married to him.

Lucy. There was not much difficulty in that; but if any thing could have frighten'd her into that belief, her filthy guardian had done it—He made her almoft believe, that the faving her foul depended upon marrying him—Did you ever hear of fuch a reprobate?

Belv. How I adore her bewitching fimplicity!

Lucy. Simplicity, Sir! fhe's able to make a fool of any of us—if I had half her wit, I would not continue long in fervice, as well as I love my miftrefs.

Belv. But, dear Lucy, what can Mifs Peggy propofe?

Lucy. To run away from her guardian, and marry you.

Belv. She might have done both, and loft the opportunity.

Lucy. She will do both, and make an opportunity, if it does not come of itfelf. The thoughts of running away, or of being married, when taken feparately, will put any maiden of us into great

5

confufion;

confufion; but when they come both together, are too much for the boldeft of us—Mifs Peggy was overpower'd with your propofal, and no wonder fhe could not determine for the beft; I fhould have been a little frighten'd myfelf.

Belv. But has the dear creature refolv'd?

Lucy. Has fhe—why, fhe will run away and marry you, in fpite of your teeth, the firft moment fhe can break prifon—fo you, in your turn, muft take care not to have your qualms—I have known feveral bold gentlemen not able to draw their fwords, when a challenge has come too quick upon 'em.

Belv. I affure you, Mrs. Lucy, that I am no bully in love, and Mifs Peggy will meet with her match, come when fhe will.

Lucy. Ay, fo you all fay, but talking does no bufinefs—ftay at home till you hear from us.

Belv. Bleffings on thee, Lucy, for the thought.

Moody *fpeaking without.*

Moody. But I muft and will fee him, let him have what company he will.

Lucy. As I hope to be marry'd, Mr. Belville, I hear Mr. Moody's voice---where fhall I hide myfelf?—if he fees me--we are all undone.

Belv. This is our curfed luck again—what the devil can he want here?——I have loft my fenfes—get into this clofet till he's gone. [*puts Lucy into the clofet.*] This vifit means fomething; I am quite confounded—Don't you ftir, Lucy—I muft put the beft face upon the matter—Now for it— [*takes a book and reads.*

Enter Moody.

Moody. You will excufe me, Sir, for breaking thro' forms, and your fervant's intreaties, to have

the

the honour---but you are alone, Sir--your fellow told me below that you were with company.

Belv. Yes, Sir, the beſt company. [*ſhews his book.*] When I converſe with my betters, I chuſe to have 'em alone.

Moody. And I choſe to interrupt your converſation ; the buſineſs of my errand muſt plead my excuſe.

Belv. You ſhall be always welcome to me—but you ſeem ruffled, Sir ; what brings you hither, and ſo ſeemingly out of humour ?

Moody. Your impertinency--I beg pardon--- your modeſty, I mean.

Belv. My impertinency !

Moody. Your impertinency.

Belv. Sir, from the peculiarity of your charaćter, and your intimacy with my uncle, I ſhall allow you great privileges : but you muſt conſider, youth has its privileges too ; and as I have not the honour of your acquaintance, I am not oblig'd to bear with your ill humours, or your ill manners.

Moody. They who wrong me, young man, muſt bear with both ; and if you had not made too free with me, I ſhould have taken no liberties with you.

Belv. I don't underſtand you, Sir ; but you gentlemen, who have handſome wives, think you have a privilege of ſaying any thing to us young fellows, and are as brutiſh as if you were our creditors.

Moody. I ſhan't truſt you any way.

Belv. But why ſo diffident, Sir ? you don't know me.

Moody. I am not diffident, young man, but certain, becauſe I think I do know you.

Belv. I could have wiſh'd, Sir, to have found you a little more civil, the firſt time I have the honour of a viſit from you.

Moody.

Moody. If that is all you want, young gentle-man, you will find me very civil indeed! There, Sir;---read that, and let your modesty declare whe-ther I want either kindness or civility---Look you there, Sir.   [*gives a letter.*

Belv. What is't?

Moody. Only a love letter, Sir;---and from my wife.

Belv. How, is it from your wife?---hum and hum.   [*reads.*

Moody. Even from my wife, Sir; am not I wond'rous kind and civil to you now too? But you'll not think her so.   [*aside.*

Belv. Ha, is this a trick of his or her's? [*aside.*

Moody. The gentleman's surpriz'd, I find; what, you expected a kinder letter?

Belv. No, faith, not I, how cou'd I?

Moody. Yes, yes, I'm sure you did; a man so young, and well made as you are, must needs be disappointed, if the women declare not their passion at the first sight, or opportunity.

Belv. But what shou'd this mean? It seems, he knows not what the letter contains!   [*aside.*

Moody. Come, ne'er wonder at it so much.

Belv. Faith, I can't help it.

Moody. Now, I think, I have deserv'd your infinite friendship and kindness, and have shew'd myself sufficiently an obliging kind friend and hus-band---am I not so, to bring a letter from my wife to her gallant?

Belv. Ay, indeed you are the most obliging kind friend and husband in the world; ha, ha, ha! Pray, however, present my humble service to her, and tell her, I will obey her letter to a tittle, and fulfil her desires, be what they will, or with what difficulty soever I do't; and you shall be no more jealous of me, I warrant her, and you.

                                                    Moody.

Moody. Well then, fare you well, and play with any man's honour but mine, kifs any man's wife but mine, and welcome---fo, Mr. Modéfty, your fervant. [*as* Moody *is going out he is met by* Sparkifh.

Spark. So, brother-in-law, that was to have been, I have follow'd you from home to Belville's: I have ftrange news for you.·

Moody. What, are you wifer than you were this morning?

Spark. Faith I don't know but I am, for I have loft your fifter, and I fhan't eat half an ounce the lefs at dinner for it; there's philofophy for you.

Moody. Infenfibility, you mean---I hope you don't mean to ufe my fifter ill, Sir?.

Spark. No, Sir, fhe has ufed me ill; fhe's in her tantrums—I have had a narrow efcape, Sir.

Moody. If thou art endow'd with the fmalleft portion of underftanding, explain this riddle.

Belv. Ay, ay, prithee, Sparkifh---condefcend to be intelligible.

Spark. Why, you muft know---we had fettled to be married---it is the fame thing to me, whether I am married or not---I have no particular fancy one way or another, and fo I told your fifter; off or on, 'tis the fame thing to me; but the thing was fix'd, you know—You and my Aunt brought it about---I had no hand in it. And, to fhew you that I was as willing to marry your fifter as any other woman, I fuffered the law to tye me up to hard terms, and the church would have finifh'd me ftill to harder---but fhe was taken with her tantrums!

Moody. Damn your tantrums---come to the point.

Spark. Your fifter took an averfion to the parfon, Frank Harcourt's brother—abus'd him like a pick-pocket, and fwore 'twas Harcourt himfelf.

Moody.

Moody. And fo it was, for I faw him.

Spark. Here's fine work!—why, you are as mad as your fifter---I tell you it was Ned, Frank's twin brother.

Moody. What, Frank told you fo?

Spark. Ay, and Ned too---they were both in a ftory.

Moody. What an incorrigible fellow!---Come, come, I muft be gone.

Spark. Nay, nay, you fhall hear my ftory out. ---She walk'd up within piftol-fhot of the church ---then twirl'd round upon her heel---call'd me every name fhe could think of; and when fhe had exhaufted her imagination, and tir'd her tongue--- no eafy matter, let me tell you---fhe call'd her chair, fent her footman to buy a monkey before my face, then bid me good-morrow with a fneer, and left us with our mouths open in the middle of a hundred people, who were all laughing at us! If thefe are not tantrums, I don't know what are.

Moody. Ha, ha, ha! I thank thee, Sparkifh, from my foul; 'tis a moft exquifite ftory; I have not had fuch a laugh for this half year---Thou art a moft ridiculous puppy, and I am infinitely oblig'd to thee; ha, ha, ha!   [*Exit Moody.*

Spark. Did you ever hear the like, Belville?

Belville. O yes; how is it poffible to hear fuch a foolifh ftory, and fee thy foolifh face, and not laugh at 'em; ha, ha, ha!

Lucy in the clofet laughs.

Spark. Hey-day! what's that? what have you rais'd a devil in the clofet, to make up a laughing chorus at me? I muft take a peep—

         [*going to the clofet.*

Belv. Indeed but you muft not.

Spark.

2

Spark. 'Twas a woman's voice.

Belv. So much the better for me.

Spark. Prithee introduce me.

Belv. Though you take a pleasure in exposing your ladies, I choose to conceal mine. So, my dear Sparkish, left the lady should be sick by too long a confinement, and laughing heartily at you ---I must intreat you to withdraw---Prithee excuse me, I must laugh---ha, ha, ha!

Spark. Do you know that I begin to be angry, Belville?

Belv. I can't help that; ha, ha, ha!

Spark. My character's at stake----I shall be. thought a damn'd filly fellow---I will call Alithea to an account directly.   [*Exit.*

Belv. Ha, ha, ha!

Lucy peeping out.

Lucy. Ha, ha, ha! O dear Sir, let me have my laugh out, or I shall burst---What an adventure! [*laughs.*

Belv. My sweet Peggy has sent me the kindest letter---and by the dragon himself---There's a spirit for you!

Lucy. There's simplicity for you! Shew me a town-bred girl with half the genius---Send you a love-letter, and by a jealous guardian too! ha, ha, ha! 'Tis too much---too much---

Belv. She begs me to stay at home---for she intends to run away with me, the first opportunity.

Lucy. And, to complete the whole, my mistress is deliver'd from her fool too---Ha, ha, ha! I shall die; ha! ha! ha!---Dear Mr. Belville, laugh, laugh, I beseech you laugh.

Belv. I do, I do, my dear Lucy, and I hope we never shall have cause to be less merry as long as we live---ha, ha, ha!

Lucy.

Lucy. O never, never---I fhall certainly die---
Well, Mr. Belville---the world goes as it fhould do
—my miftrefs will exchange her fool for a wit,
Mifs Peggy her brute for a pretty young fellow ;
I fhall dance at two weddings---be well rewarded
by both parties---get a hufband myfelf, and be
as happy as the beft of you---and fo your humble
fervant.   [*Exit.*

Belv. Succefs attend you, Lucy—   [*Exit,*

THE END OF THE FOURTH ACT.

ACT V.

SCENE Moody's *house*.

Miss Peggy *alone, leaning on her elbow. A table, pen, ink, and paper.*

Peg. WELL, 'tis e'en so, I have got the London disease they call love ; I am sick of my guardian, and dying for Mr. Belville! I have heard this distemper call'd a fever, but methinks it is liker an ague ; for, when I think of my guardian, I tremble, and am in a cold sweat ; but when I think of my gallant, dear Mr. Belville, my hot fit comes, and I am all in a fever indeed : my own chamber is tedious to me, and I would fain be remov'd to his, and then methinks I shou'd be very well. Ah! poor Mr. Belville! Well, I cannot, will not stay here ; therefore I'll make an end of my letter to him, which shall be a finer letter than my last, because I have studied it like any thing. Oh! sick, sick!

Enter Moody, *who seeing her writing, steals softly behind her, and looking over her shoulder, snatches the paper from her.*

Moody. What, writing more letters ?

Peg. O Lord! Bud, why d'ye fright me so ?
    [*she offers to run out, he stops her and reads.*

Moody. How's this ! nay, you shall not stir, Madam. *Dear, dear, dear Mr. Belville,*---very well, I have taught you to write letters to good purpose---but let's see't.---[*reads.*]---*First, I am to beg your pardon for my boldness in writing to you, which I'd have you to know I would not have done, bad you not said first you lov'd me so extremely ; which,*

F   *if*

if you do, you will never suffer me to be another man's, who I loath, naufeate, and deteft: (now you can write thefe filthy words.)   But what follows?---*therefore, I hope you will fpeedily find fome way to free me from this unfortunate match, which was never, I affure you, of my choice, but I'm afraid 'tis already too far gone; however, if you love me, as I do you, you will try what you can do; you muft help me away before to-morrow, or elfe, alas! I fhall be for ever out of your reach, for I can defer no longer our*---our---(what is to follow our---fpeak what) our journey into the country, I fuppofe.--- Oh, woman, damn'd woman! and Love, damn'd Love! their old tempter; for this is one of his miracles: in a moment he can make thofe blind that cou'd fee, and thofe fee that were blind; thofe dumb that could fpeak, and thofe prattle who were dumb before; nay, what is more than all, make thofe dough-bak'd, fenfelefs, indocile animals, women, too hard for us, their politick lords and rulers, in a moment.   But make an end of your letter, and then I'll make an end of you thus, and all my plagues together. [*draws his fword.*

Peg. O Lord! O Lord! you are fuch a paf- fionate man, Bud!

Moody. Come, take the pen, and make an end of the letter, juft as you intended; if you are falfe in a tittle, I fhall foon perceive it, and punifh you with this, as you deferve. [*lays his hand on his fword.*]   Write what was to follow---let's fee--- (*You muft make hafte and help me away before to- morrow, or elfe I fhall be for ever out of your reach, for I can defer no longer our*) what follows our?---
                [*Peggy takes the pen and writes.*

Peg. Muft all out then, Bud?---Look you there, then.

Moody. Let's fee---(*for I can defer no longer our wedding---Your flighted Alithea.*) What's the mean-

3   ing

ing of this, my fifter's name to't? fpeak, un-
riddle.

Peg. Yes, indeed, Bud.

Moody. But why her name to't? fpeak---fpeak,
I fay.

Peg. Ay, but you'll tell her again : if you wou'd
not tell her again---

Moody. I will not ; I am ftunn'd, my head turns
round. Speak.

Peg. Won't you tell her indeed, and indeed?

Moody. No ; fpeak, I fay.

Peg. She'll be angry with me ; but I had rather
fhe fhould be angry with me than you, Bud. And
to tell you the truth, 'twas fhe made me write the
letter, and taught me what I fhould write.

Moody. Ha---I thought the ftyle was fomewhat
better than her own. [*afide.*] Cou'd fhe come to
you to teach you, fince I had lock'd you up alone?

Peg. Oh, thro' the key-hole, Bud.

Moody. But why fhou'd fhe make you write a
letter for her to him, fince fhe can write herfelf?

Peg. Why, fhe faid becaufe---for I was unwilling to do it.

Moody. Becaufe, what---becaufe---

Peg. Becaufe, left Mr. Belville, as he was fo
young, fhou'd be inconftant and refufe her, or be
vain afterwards, and fhew the letter, fhe might
difown it, the hand not being hers.

Moody. Belville again!---Am I to be deceiv'd
again with that young hypocrite?

Peg. You have deceiv'd yourfelf, Bud, you
have indeed---I have kept the fecret, for my fifter's
fake, as long as I could---but you muft know it---
and fhall know it too. [*cries.*

Moody. Dry your eyes.

Peg. You always thought he was hankering after
me---Good law! he's dying for Alithea, and Alithea for him---they have had private meetings---

and

and he was making love to her before yefterday, from the tavern window, when you thought it was to me---I would have difcover'd all---but fhe made me fwear to deceive you, and fo I have finely--- have not I, Bud?

Moody. Why did you write that foolifh letter to him then, and make me more foolifh to carry it?

Peg. To carry on the joke, Bud---to oblige them.

Moody. And will nothing ferve her but that taper jackanapes, that great baby?---he's too young for her to marry.

Peg. Why do you marry me then? 'tis the fame thing, Bud.

Moody. No, no, 'tis quite different---How innocent fhe is!---This changeling cou'd not invent this lye; but if fhe cou'd, why fhou'd fhe? fhe might think I fhould foon difcover it. [*afide.*]---But hark you, Madam, your fifter went out in the morning, and I have not feen her within fince.

Peg. Alack-a-day, fhe has been crying all day above, it feems, in a corner.

Moody. Where is fhe? let me fpeak with her.

Peg. O Lord! then fhe'll difcover all---[*afide.*] Pray hold, Bud; what d'ye mean to difcover me! fhe'll know I have told you then. Pray, Bud, let me talk with her firft.

Moody. I muft fpeak with her, to know whether Belville ever made her any promife, and whether fhe will be marry'd to Sparkifh, or no.

Peg. Pray, dear Bud, don't, till I have fpoken with her, and told her that I have told you all; for fhe'll kill me elfe.

Moody. Go then, and bid her come to me.

Peg. Yes, yes, Bud.

Moody. Let me fee---

Peg.

Peg. I have juſt got time to know of Lucy, who firſt ſet me on work, what lye I ſhall tell next; for I am e'en at my wits end. [*Exit* Peggy.

Moody. Well, I reſolve it, Belville ſhall have her: I'd rather give him my ſiſter, than lend him my wife; and ſuch an alliance will prevent his pretenſions to my wife, ſure---I'll make him of kin to her, and then he won't care for her.

Enter Miſs Peggy.

Peg. O Lord, Bud, I told you what anger you wou'd make me with my ſiſter.

Moody. Won't ſhe come hither?

Peg. No, no, ſhe's aſham'd to look you in the face; ſhe'll go directly to Mr. Belville, ſhe ſays--- She muſt ſpeak with him, before ſhe diſcovers all to you---or even ſees you---She ſays too, that you ſhall know the reaſon by-and-by---Pray let her have her way, Bud---ſhe won't be pacify'd if you don't---and will never forgive me---For my part, Bud, I believe, but don't tell any body, they have broken a piece of ſilver between 'em---or have contracted one another, as we have done, you know, which is the next thing to being marry'd.

Moody. Pooh! you fool---ſhe aſham'd of talking with me about Belville, becauſe I made the match for her with Sparkiſh! But Sparkiſh is a fool, and I have no objection to Belville's family or fortune---tell her ſo.

Peg. I will, Bud. [*going.*

Moody. Stay, ſtay, Peggy---let her have her own way---ſhe ſhall go to Belville herſelf, and I'll follow her---that will be beſt---let her have her whim.

Peg. You're in the right, Bud---for they have certainly had a quarrel, by her crying and hanging her head ſo---I'll be hang'd if her eyes an't

ſwell'd

fwell'd out of her head, fhe's in fuch a piteous taking.

Moody. Belville fhan't ufe her ill, I'll take care of that---if he has made her a promife, he fhall keep to it---but fhe had better go firft---a word or two by themfelves will clear matters for my appearance---I will follow her at a diftance, that fhe may have no interruption; and I will wait in the Park before I fee them, that they may come to a reconciliation before I come upon 'em.

Peg. Law, Bud, how wife you are! I wifh I had half your wifdom; you fee every thing at once--- Stand a one fide then---and I'll tell her you are gone to your room, and when fhe paffes by, you may follow her.

Moody. And fo I will---fhe fhan't fee me till I break in upon her at Belville's.

Peg. Now for it.   [*Exit Mifs* Peggy.

Moody. My cafe is fomething better---for fuppofe the worft---fhould Belville ufe her ill---I had rather fight him for not marrying my fifter, than for debauching my wife, for I will make her mine abfolutely to-morrow; and of the two, I had rather find my fifter too forward than my wife: I expected no other from her free education, as fhe calls it, and her paffion for the town---Well, wife and fifter are names which make us expect love and duty, pleafure and comfort; but we find 'em plagues and torments, and are equally, tho' differently, troublefome to their keeper. But here fhe comes.   [*fteps on one fide.*

Enter Mifs Peggy, *drefs'd like* Alithea; *and as fhe paffes over the ftage, feems to figh, fob, and wipe her eyes.*

Peg. Heigho!   [*Exit.*

Moody. [*comes forward.*] There the poor devil goes, fighing and fobbing; a woeful example of the fatal confequences of a town education---but I am bound in duty, as well as inclination, to do my utmoft to fave her---but firft I'll fecure my own property. [*opens the door and calls*]---Peggy! Peggy!---my dear!---I will return as foon as poffible, do you hear me? Why don't you anfwer? You may read in the book I bought you 'till I come back---As the Jew fays in the play, faft bind, faft find.. [*locks the door.*] This is the beft, and only fecurity for female affections. [*Exit, holding up the key.*

Scene the Park before Belville's *door.*

Enter Sparkifh---*fuddled.*

Spark. If I can but meet with her, or any body that belongs to her, they will find me a match for 'em---When a man has wit, and a great deal of it ---Champagne gives it a double edge, and nothing can withftand it---'tis a lighted match to gunpowder---the mine is fprung, and the poor devils are tofs'd heels uppermoft in an inftant. I was right to confult my friends, and they all agree with Moody, that I make a damn'd ridiculous figure, as matters ftand at prefent. I'll confult Belville---this is his houfe, he's my friend too---and no fool---It fhall be fo---damn it, I muft not be ridiculous. [*going to the door, fees* Peggy *coming.*] Hold! hold! if the Champagne does not hurt my eye-fight, while it fharpens my wit, the enemy is marching up this way---Come on, Madam Alithea; now for a fmart fire, and then let's fee who will be ridiculous.

Enter Mifs Peggy.

Peg. Dear me, I begin to tremble---there is Mr. Sparkifh, and I can't get to Mr. Belville's houfe without paffing by him---he fees me---and

will

will difcover me----he feems in liquor too!---blefs me.

Spark. Oho! fhe ftands at bay a little---fhe don't much relifh the engagement---The firft blow is half the battle---I'll be a little figurative with her. [*approaching her.*] I find, Madam, you like a folo better than a duet. You need not have been walking alone this evening, if you had been wifer yefterday---What nothing to fay for yourfelf?---Repentance, I fuppofe, makes you as aukward and as foolifh, as the poor country girl your brother has lock'd up in Pall-Mall.

Peg. I'm frighten'd out of my wits.   [*tries to pafs by him.*

Spark. Not a ftep farther fhall you go, 'till you give me an account of your behaviour, and make me reparation for being ridiculous. What, dumb ftill!---then if you won't by fair means, I muft fqueeze you to a confeffion. [*as he goes to feize her, fhe flips by him---but he catches hold of her before fhe reaches* Belville's *door.*] Not quite fo faft, if you pleafe---Come, come---let me fee your modeft face, and hear your foft tongue---or I fhall be tempted to ufe you ill.

Enter Moody.

Moody. Hands off, you ruffian---how dare you ufe a lady, and my fifter in this manner? [Moody *takes her from* Sparkifh.

Spark. She's my property, Sir---transfer'd to me by you---and tho' I would give her up to any body for a dirty fword-knot, yet I won't be bullied out of my right, tho' it is not worth that---[*fnaps his fingers.*

Moody. There's a fellow to be a hufband---you are juftify'd in defpifing him, and flying from him ---I'll defend you with my purfe and my fword---knock at that door, and let me fpeak to Belville.---

[Peggy

[Peggy *knocks at the door, when the servant opens it, she runs in.*]---Is your master at home, friend?

Serv. Yes, Sir.

Moody. Tell him then, that I have rescu'd that lady from this gentleman, and that by her desire, and my consent, she flies to him for protection; if he can get a parson, let him marry her this minute; tell him so, and shut the door.

Serv. And that he will, I'll answer for him.

[*Exit.*

Spark. The man's mad, stark mad!

Moody. And now, Sir, if your wine has given you courage, you had better shew it upon this occasion, for you are still damn'd ridiculous.

Spark. Did you ever hear the like---Look ye, Mr. Moody, we are in the Park, and to draw a sword is an offence to the court---so you may vapour as long as you please. A woman of so little taste, is not worth fighting for---she's not worth my sword; but if you'll fight me to-morrow morning for diversion, I am your man.

Moody. Relinquish your title in the lady to Belville peaceably, and you may sleep in a whole skin.

Spark. Belville! he would not have your sister, with the fortune of a nabob; no, no, his mouth waters at your country tid-bit at home---much good may do him.

Moody. And you think so, puppy—ha, ha, ha!

Spark. Yes, I do, mastiff---ha, ha, ha!

Moody. Then thy folly is complete—ha, ha, ha!

Spark. Thine will be so, when thou hast married thy country innocence—ha, ha, ha! [*they laugh at each other.*

Enter Harcourt.

Moody. Who have we here?

Spark. What, my boy Harcourt!

Moody.

Moody. What brings you here, Sir?

Harc. I follow'd you to Belville's, to prefent a near relation of yours, and a nearer one of mine, to you.

Spark. What's the matter now?

Enter a chair, with Alithea.

Harc. [*takes her by the hand.*] Give me leave, gentlemen, without offence to either, to prefent Mrs. Harcourt to you!

Spark. Alithea! your wife! --Mr. Moody, are you in the clouds too?

Moody. If I am not in a dream---I am the moft miferable waking dog, that ever run mad with his misfortunes and aftonifhment!

Harc. Why fo, Jack---can you object to my happinefs, when this gentleman was unworthy of it?

Alith. Nothing but his total indifference to me, and the higheft opinion of himfelf, could poffibly have forc'd me to fly here for protection. [*pointing to* Harcourt. Moody *walking about in a rage.*

Spark. This is very fine, very fine, indeed--- where's your ftory about Belville now, fquire Moody? Prithee don't chafe and ftare, and ftride, and beat thy head like a mad tragedy poet---but out with thy tropes and figures.

Moody. Zounds! I can't bear it. [*goes haftily to* Belville's *door and knocks hard.*

Alith. Dear brother, what's the matter?

Moody. The devil's the matter! the devil and woman together. [*knocks again.*] I'll break the door down, if they won't anfwer. [*knocks again.*

Serv. [*at the balcony.*] What would your honour pleafe to have?

Moody. Your mafter, rafcal!

Serv. He is obeying your commands, Sir, and the moment he has finifh'd, he will do himfelf the pleafure to wait on you.

Moody.

Moody. You fneering villain you---if your mafter does not produce that fhe-devil, who is now with him, and who, with a face of innocence, has cheated and undone me, I'll fet fire to his houfe.

[*Exit Servant.*

Spark. Gad fo! now I begin to fmoke the bufinefs. Well faid, fimplicity, rural fimplicity! egad! if thou haft trick'd Cerberus here, I fhall be fo ravifh'd, that I will give this couple a wedding dinner. Pray, Mr. Moody, who's damn'd ridiculous now?

Moody. [*going to* Sparkifh.] Look ye, Sir--- don't grin, for if you dare to fhew your teeth at my misfortunes---I'll dafh 'em down your impudent throat, you jackanapes.

Spark. [*quite calm.*] Very fine, faith---but I have no weapons to butt with a mad bull, fo you may tofs and roar by yourfelf, if you pleafe.

Belville *appears in the balcony.*

Belv. What does my good friend want with me?

Moody. Are you a villain, or are you not?

Belv. I have obey'd your commands, Sir.

Moody. What have you done with the girl, Sir?

Belv. Made her my wife, as you defired.

Spark. Very true, I am your witnefs---'tis pleafant, faith; ha, ha, ha! [*laughs to himfelf.*

Moody. She's my wife, and I demand her.

Peggy *appears in the balcony.*

Peg. No, but I an't---what's the matter, Bud, are you angry with me?

Moody. How dare you look me in the face, cockatrice?

Peg. How dare you look me in the face, Bud? Have you not given me to another, when you ought to have married me yourfelf? Have not you

pretended

pretended to be married to me, when you knew in your confcience you was not?---And have not you been fhilly fhally for a long time? So that if I had not married dear Mr. Belville, I fhould not have married at all---fo I fhould not.

Spark. Extremely pleafant, faith; ha, ha, ha!

Moody. I'am ftupify'd with fhame, rage, and aftonifhment---my fate has o'ercome me---I can ftruggle no more with it. [*fighs.*] What is left me?---I cannot bear to look, or be look'd upon.--- I will hurry down to my old houfe; take a twelve-month's provifion into it---cut down my draw-bridge, run wild about my garden, which fhall grow as wild as myfelf---then will I curfe the world, and every individual in it---and when my rage and fpirits fail me, I will be found dead among the nettles and thiftles; a woeful example of the bafenefs and treachery of one fex, and of the falfe-hood, lying perjury, deceit, impudence and--- damnation of the other. [*Exit.*

Mr. and Mrs. Belville *leave the balcony.*

Spark. Very droll, and extravagantly comic, I muft confefs; ha, ha, ha!

Enter Mr. and Mrs. Belville.

Spark. Look ye, Belville, I wifh you joy with all my heart---you have got the prize, and perhaps have caught a tartar---that's no bufinefs of mine--- If you want evidence for Mr. Moody's giving his confent to your marriage, I fhall be ready. I bear no ill will to that pair, I wifh you happy---[*to Mr. and Mrs.* Harcourt]---tho' I'm fure they'll be miferable---and fo your humble fervant. [*Exit.*

Mrs. Belv. I hope you forgive me, Alithea, for playing your brother this trick; indeed I fhould have only made him and myfelf miferable, had we married together.

Alith.

Alith. Then 'tis much better.as it is---But I am yet in the dark, how this matter has been brought about. How your innocence, my dear, has out-witted his worldly wifdom.

Belv. If you will walk in, Madam, for a moment, we will tell your our adventure, and confult with you and Mr. Harcourt, the moft likely means to reconcile your brother to us---we will be guided by you in every ftep we take.

Alith. And we fhall be ready and happy to effect fo defirable an end.

Mrs. Belv. I am fure I'll do any thing to pleafe my Bud but marry him.

[*She comes forward, and addreffes the audience in the following* EPILOGUE.]

BUT you, good Gentry, what fay you to this?
You are to judge me---have I done amifs?
I've Reafons will convince you all, and ftrong ones,
Except Old Folks, who hanker after young ones;
Bud was fo paffionate, and grown fo thrifty,
'Twas a fad Life!---and then, he was near fifty!
I'm but nineteen---my Hufband too is young,
So foft, fo gentle, fuch a winning tongue! }
Have I, pray Ladies fpeak, done very wrong?
As for poor Bud, 'twas honeft to deceive him!
More vartuous fure to cheat him, than to grieve him.
Great Folk, I know, will call me fimple Slut,
Marry for Love! they cry, the Country Put,

Marriage with them's a Fashion---soon grows cool:
But I'm for loving always, like a Fool.
With half my Fortune, I would rather part,
Than be all Finery, with an aching Heart.
For these strange aukward Notions don't abuse me ;
And, as I know no better---pray excuse me.

F I N I S.